DRAGON'S NANNY

DRAGON DREAMS 3

LEELA ASH

TABITHA ST. GEORGE

Dragon's Nanny

Join the Totally Romance Facebook Group!

https://www.totallyromancebooks.com/leela-ash

CONTENTS

CHAPTER 1

The house wasn't the scariest thing Ariel McDunnah had ever seen... but it came close.

From the moment her chauffeur turned onto the elm-lined drive, her stomach sank. Lower and lower it went as acres of neatly trimmed lawns and hedges scrolled past. A barn and full equestrian arena on the left. Four tennis courts on the right.

By the time the mansion came in sight, with its white pillared porch and a swimming pool the size of a small lake, Ariel was ready to jump out of the car and flee.

I do not *belong here!*

Oblivious to her fear, the driver pulled up in front of this palace. Its great oak doors swung open and a portly man in a neat uniform emerged.

There was a word for men like that. She wracked her memories of old British tv shows, struggling to find it. Butler? Valet? Were those two different things? How did you tell them apart?

With a click, the chauffeur swept her door open, leaving

her no choice except to emerge from the safety of the town car.

"Miss McDunnah? Welcome to Windhope Hall."

The house had its own *name*? One hand dropped to the side of her Goodwill dress and brushed at it, as if she hoped it could brush her invisible. Once more, she wondered why on earth she'd come.

"Thank you."

"This way, please. I'm George Summers."

Still no answer to the 'butler/valet' conundrum. Ariel followed him meekly through the double doors, down a polished marble hall, and to a sunny sitting room filled with flowers. In the distance, she heard children's laughter. That sound – the first normal thing in this terrifyingly elegant place – gave her a touch of relief.

"Have a seat, please. Master Jackson is... delayed."

Was it her imagination, or did his eyes narrow in disproval? She didn't know. She also didn't know if it was Mr. Jackson's tardiness or her dull, frumpy clothes that annoyed George.

Well, she wasn't going to worry about it. That way led to paranoia and if she got any more nervous, she'd make herself sick.

"Tea?"

She shook her head.

"Coffee? Water?"

Two more shakes.

Now his lips definitely did grow pinched. "Very well. Let's get to business then, shall we? I believe you have a letter of recommendation?"

"Oh! Yes, of course!" From within her purse she produced a parchment letter covered in elegant script. It was slightly rumpled; in her nervousness, she'd throttled it a bit.

George took it from her, smoothed it with a faint frown, then read silently.

"Brandon Lorde sent you." Despite his reserve, one eyebrow rose. Few Shifters were as famous as the Alpha of the Dragons' First Flight. "Impressive. Have you known him long?"

"No," she had to admit. "I've never met Mr. Lorde. However, my parents knew him well."

"I see." Some of his approval evaporated. "Your parents were Bear Shifters, yes?"

"Yes. They died last year."

She could say that now and stay dry-eyed. When a hurricane threatened the town they warded, her parents had driven their boat, time and again, into the teeth of the storm. Two dozen people were snatched from the rising water. Two dozen lives saved. But that wasn't good enough for them. Bears to the end, they went back one more time, fighting to reach an isolated nursing home.

They never came back.

They were heroes.

Unlike her.

Ariel wasn't a Shifter. Mom and Dad never said a word about that, but she knew that it broke their hearts when her first moon's time came and she didn't Shift. They never called her a 'failure' but she knew better. She was just Kin. Useless. Always the protected, never the Protector. When the skies grew black and wind tore the trees from the ground, they sent her with the other evacuees. She'd cried, demanded they let her help. They refused. And when, in the end, she wouldn't accept that, they told her the ugly truth.

She wouldn't be any help. She'd be a burden.

Those were their last words. That was how they parted, forever.

"Miss McDunnah?"

George's voice dragged her away from those despairing thoughts. Ariel found the man staring at her in annoyance. "Yes?"

"I *asked* what your qualifications were."

"Oh. Yes. Right." Her cheeks burned and she licked her lips. "I have an Associate of Child Care degree and two years experience in a nursery school."

"Did you care for younger siblings?"

"No, I was an only child."

"I see." Clearly, her limited experience did not impress him. "What, precisely, makes you believe you're qualified to care for the children of a Dragon?"

She'd prepared for this question. Dragons were the princes of the Shifter world, the strongest, most noble, most powerful of the Shifting kind. Only a handful remained now. Caring for a Dragon's children was a calling worthy of a full Bear.

So why should she, a mere Kin, think she deserved a chance like this?

Suddenly, all of her carefully crafted responses vanished. Ariel sat, mind blank. Seconds ticked past, painfully long in the silence. Finally, she blurted out the only thing that came to mind: "I, uh, I like children. A lot."

George didn't even need to sneer 'I see' again. The disdain was far too plain in his face.

Seriously? 'I like kids.' As if no one else on the planet likes them too?

Oh, she was an idiot for thinking she ever had a shot at this job! Ariel's gaze fell to the floor, and now, the first sting of tears burned in her eyes. No skills, no experience. Even her recommendation was second-hand. Brandon Lorde just wanted to repay her parents.

As she opened her mouth to apologize, however, the front

door slammed open. A second later, a man bounded into the sitting room – and Ariel's heart skipped a beat.

Skin-tight jeans and a tight t-shirt showed off every muscle in his tall, athletic body. Ripped calves, six-pack abs, and a tight, hot…

Her cheeks burned again and she quickly tore her eyes away from his buttocks. Ogling your prospective employer was *not* a good way to get a job! (Even if it was so terribly tempting.)

"Heya, George!"

"Mister Jackson."

So, this was a Dragon? He was more slender than she'd imagined. Bears like her father tended to be heavy-set and she'd expected something like that. Owen Jackson, however, looked like a sprinter, not a linebacker. Rangy, lean, and powerful.

"This is Miss Ariel McDunnah. She's applying for the position of nanny."

"Pleasure to meet you." He held a hand out to her.

Ariel took it, glanced up… and found herself lost again.

Emerald green eyes, bright as gems, studied her. They sparkled with an impish glee. A smile hovered over his lips, barely controlled, as if he might burst into laughter at any moment. She barely noticed the other details: his high cheekbones and rakish brown hair. Those eyes captivated her. They whispered promises. Wicked pleasures. A world of delicious, dangerous fun.

Flustered, she let her hand drop back into her lap. What on earth made her think all that? She wasn't a woman who gaped at men, but the energy, the barely-controlled excitement that radiated from him, left her speechless.

Fortunately, he didn't expect her to say anything. He pounced on her reference letter. "Brandon Lorde sent you? Nice!"

"Thank you," she managed to murmur.

One quick scan and then the letter, already forgotten, dropped from his fingers back onto the desk. "When can you start?"

Start? She had the job? Ariel was too stunned to say a word.

George, however, was just annoyed. "Mr. Jackson," he huffed as he scooped up the discarded reference, "Miss McDunnah is the first applicant."

That devilish grin she'd sensed finally broke free. "Early bird gets the worm, right?"

She had *no* idea what to say to that!

"We should interview at least a few others!" the other man protested.

Owen shot him an incredulous look. "Why would I want a slow nanny?"

"Speed is *not* one of a nanny's prime duties," George muttered.

"Have you seen how Trey and Brody tear around this place? I have. I'm going with the fast nanny. When can you start?"

Ariel suspected he was just teasing now, but the exchange gave her a second to recover from the shock of being handed this dream job. "I guess any time."

"So 'now' would work? Great!" he exclaimed, before she had a chance to protest. "Because I need a nanny right now."

"Mr. Jackson!" cried the exasperated George. "There *are* some concerns with Miss McDunnah's inexperience."

The delight in Owen's eyes cooled. "Are you telling me that you think my Alpha recommended a bad nanny?"

"No, no, certainly not, but…"

"Because if you are, I can tell him that. I'm flying out to meet him in an hour."

Ariel shivered at the veiled threat in those words.

Note to self: 'Mister' Jackson doesn't like to be questioned. He may not be the easiest person to work with...

"No, I'm sure Miss McDunnah will do fine," George gulped.

As soon as he got his way, Owen's high spirits returned. "Great! Come with me and I'll introduce you to the kids."

"Wonderful." She prayed her voice didn't betray her doubt – but now she was genuinely worried. Ariel was only Kin, not a true Bear. Yet, she'd been raised by Bears. Bear blood flowed through her veins. And nothing was as important to that Kind as family.

How could he entrust his family to a woman he's never met? He didn't even ask me any questions!

Much as she hated it, she was with George on this one. Owen Jackson was *not* showing due diligence.

Unlike George, though, she knew she was qualified, even if she didn't have extensive experience. She was Bear-kin. She would take good care of these children. It would all work out in the end.

With long strides, Owen headed down the hall. Ariel had to trot to keep up. They came to an entertainment room with a tv the size of a movie screen. One entire wall was glass and looked out over an enormous pool.

Two small boys, perhaps five and eight, splashed happily in the shallow end. "Those two little hellions are Trey and Brody," he explained.

Her unease grew. "Shouldn't they be supervised while they swim?"

"Their sister Sydnee is watching them."

He pointed at a thin child curled up in a lounge chair. Enraptured by a cell phone, she completely ignored her two brothers.

Owen leaned close and whispered, "Sydnee is great.

Really low maintenance. As long as she's got bars on her phone, you won't even know she's there."

Who on earth boasted that their kids were 'low-maintenance'? Ariel bristled at the word. Yet, she recalled how poorly Mr. Jackson had reacted to George's mild protest.

If he doesn't like being questioned, I'm sure *he hates being reprimanded!*

Nope, criticizing her employer would only earn her a quick trip to the door. She wanted this job, badly. Even more now, after seeing the children.

They needed her.

So, as unnatural as it felt, she held her tongue.

Owen didn't notice her silence at all. He was too busy giving her a quick rundown on the household. "George, you've met. There's a cook and a maid. He can introduce them."

He waved vaguely. Ariel suspected he didn't even know those people's names.

"Any questions?"

"Is there a Mrs. Jackson?"

He blinked – then burst out laughing. "Oh, hell no. I'm not the marrying kind."

At the sound of his laughter, the two boys glanced up and waved frantically. Owen gave them a cheery salute in return. Sydnee shot him one cool, disapproving stare then turned her attention back to the phone.

That child was going to require a little extra love and care, Ariel told herself.

"Their mother and I hooked up a few times. Fun girl. She ended up getting addicted to meth, though, and wound up in prison."

Not a cheery story. "Then you got the children?"

"No, her dad took them for five years. Then he had a heart-attack a month ago. Died."

There wasn't a trace of sorrow in his voice. He told the story coolly, as if he'd read it in the news.

Not as if this dreadful loss had happened to his own children.

The urge to smack her employer in the back of the head grew. Sternly, Ariel reminded herself that it could be worse. He could have abandoned his children to foster care. He might have shirked his duties for years but at least he honored them in the end.

Kind of.

Somewhere in the distance, she heard the unmistakable thrum of a helicopter.

"Oh hell," Owen groaned. "That's my ride. Sorry to run like this. I'll be back in three days, tops."

He was leaving? Already? Before even fully introducing her new charges? "But my clothes, my things, are back at the hotel..."

"George will handle that." He turned to leave.

"But I didn't bring much from Louisiana!"

"Tell George to get you new things."

Her head whirled as her world was suddenly flipped upside down. "But...!"

One of the boys – Trey? Brody? – hauled himself out of the pool and went sprinting for the diving board.

Instinct kicked in. "Hey, hey, hey!" she cried as she dashed out to the pool's edge. "No running! If you fall on this concrete you'll hurt yourself badly."

All three children froze and stared at this new, unexpected interruption. Ariel turned back towards the house, hoping that Owen would introduce her properly.

The Dragon was already gone.

Sighing, she turned back to the children. "Hello. I'm Ariel. I'm your new nanny."

No one looked impressed.

CHAPTER 2

*B*randon Lorde's San Francisco penthouse boasted a breath-taking view. Barely a stone's throw away, the Bay Bridge soared across to Oakland. Little cousin to the Golden Gate Bridge, its grey arches mirrored the curves of its more famous relative.

Owen Jackson barely noticed. His summons had thrown him into a fever of anticipation.

For centuries, magic had been lost to the world. The Wellsprings, enchanted portals that connected this world to the mystical Other Side, closed for reasons no one understood. Shifters like Owen, people whose souls were inseparably tied to the great spirits of the Other Side, held onto scraps of power. But locked away from the source of myth and wonder, the world grew cold and rational.

Two years ago, a dormant Wellspring awakened. Once again, magic flowed into the world from this one fragile, sacred site. As a Dragon, Owen knew exactly what that meant.

War.

When magic failed, Shifters failed with it. Oh, some

remembered their purpose and stayed true to it. There were still packs of Wolves who roamed the land, wild and free. A handful of Bears protected great families, the wise matriarchs and patriarchs who shielded generations. Yet, many Shifters fell into despair as the Wellsprings died. They buried themselves in empty pleasures, in drink and drugs. Dragons were hit the hardest, since it was their duty to protect the Wellsprings. Those who fell became Worms, fallen creatures that gnawed their own wings off.

Owen's Flight had remained pure, under the guidance of his Alpha, Brandon Lorde. Now, their faith had been rewarded: once more, the Flight had a living Wellspring to guard.

And, he knew, the Worms would not tolerate that. Worms had gathered the most debased Shifters into a group called 'The Fangs of Apophis.' Rumors swirled about the renewed Wellspring. Owen had no doubt that the Fangs would give, literally, anything to find it and either destroy it or twist it in their greed.

In his mind, the rebirth of the Wellspring should have triggered an immediate attack. For two years, he'd stewed, seething with impatience, while Lorde did nothing. Why? Why didn't his Flight assault the Fangs? Why didn't they take the battle to their enemies instead of hiding?

Finally, today, the summons had come, and he knew what this meant. The years of thumb twiddling, of sitting idle while their enemies grew stronger, were over. The rest of his Flight would shake off their torpor.

Lost in thoughts of revenge and glory, he followed the maître-de blindly into a luxurious wood-paneled room. His Alpha, Brandon Lorde, gazed out over the city of San Francisco, a glass of claret in his hand. Broad-shouldered, with a chiseled face and piercing gaze, he was everything a Dragon ought to be. Owen felt his chest swell with pride. There was no man he'd rather follow into battle.

"Jackson."

"Lorde."

Brandon might be his Alpha but they were both Dragons. There would be no honorifics, no tokens of subservience, between them.

"Wine?"

"Please." A waiter whisked over at once with a second glass of crimson liquid. Owen raised it in salute. "To your new Wellspring!"

"To the Wellspring." Lorde took a sip then raised the goblet again. "And to my new child and my Mate, the first woman to pass the Rite of Claiming since the Wellspring vanished ages ago."

Less exciting, but he still saluted that.

"Speaking of which, how are your own children?"

"Great!"

"I'm pleased that you decided to take charge of them."

Yeah, well, when your Alpha tells you to do something, you do it.

Dragons didn't demand subservience from their Flights – but only a fool thought he was his Alpha's equal.

Not that he was going to say that. Owen just smiled and took another gulp of the wine.

"How are they handling their grandfather's death?"

Weird. Lorde usually cut straight to business. "As well as they can, I guess. They seem to like their new home."

"Children are very resilient. I thought the boys would prosper, but I have concerns about your daughter. She's old enough that this will be hard on her."

"Sydnee? Pfft, no! She's doing great."

"I see."

That niggling doubt in Lorde's tone was starting to grate

on his nerves. Owen decided to turn the conversation away from kids. "Thanks for the nanny recommendation. Great idea. I can really use the help."

Lorde's eyes grew clouded as he swirled his wine. "She comes from an honorable family."

"Yeah, she seems great."

"Well, I'm pleased that everything is so *'great.'* "

Okay, now that definitely *was* sarcasm. Somewhere inside himself, Owen felt his Dragon stir with irritation. He knew what Lorde was on about, but no Dragon tolerated being nipped.

Enough 'pleasantries' already. Owen put his glass down and folded his arms across his chest. "I'm sure you didn't summon me to talk about nannies, though."

"No, I did not. Your Flight requires your aid. The time has come to reclaim the world."

There! *That* was the man he'd give his life for! Elation swept through him and set his heart racing.

"You have a task to set me?"

"I do. One that will, unfortunately, require some travel."

Visions of glory swam before him. Where would Lorde send him? To the Greek Isles, where they suspected the Fangs of Apophis built their lair? To the deserts of Mexico, where the rejects of a dozen Wolf bands lurked, modern-day bandits and drug runners? Or did some threat simmer closer at hand?

"Not a problem. Send me anywhere."

"Good. I need you to go to Siskiyou County, California."

That meant nothing to Owen. "What's going on there?"

"There's a Warren of Witch Hares working out of a small town called Adeline."

Magic? Owen's eyes glittered. Witch Hares weren't warriors but their spells were one of the few things that actually could hurt a Dragon. Even during the Great

Drought, when the Wellsprings lay dormant, you bearded a Hare in her lair at your peril. Now that the world's magic strengthened… who knew what they were capable of?

Well, he'd find out. "I'm on it. They'll be dead within the week."

One of Lorde's eyebrows arched. "I hope not. They're on *our* side."

"Oookay… then why am I going there?"

"They're researching a dormant Wellspring north of Mt. Shasta. Trying to find a way to awaken it. Currently, we only have one live Well, and that's a perilous situation."

"And…?" He didn't know anything about magic!

"And they may need help. You'll be the liaison between the Warren and our Flight. You'll answer to their Queen and give her any aid she requests."

His Alpha wanted him to babysit bunnies?

Owen's face fell as his dreams of battle came crashing down. He was to be a flunky, a servant – not a warrior?

It was too much. Deep inside him, his Dragon roused in anger. Its energy surged in his soul and his emerald eyes suddenly blazed with green fire. "What?" he snapped. Fury echoed in that one word, the rage that a Great Serpent felt when it was mocked.

Lorde ignored his outrage. "Do you want to know why? What your true mission is?"

That response knocked his Dragon back on its haunches. The scales which had started to spring up on his arms faded away and Owen flushed, embarrassed to have snarled at his Alpha like that. Of course, the babysitting job was a sham. Probably the Fangs had infiltrated the Warren and he needed to uncover evidence of that.

Before he killed the villains.

Hoping to cover his mistake, he nodded and took another sip of wine.

"I need you to find a Mate."

No rage this time. Both Owen and his Dragon were too shocked to react.

His Alpha meant to marry him off?

For a long moment, the two Dragons simply stared at each other. Finally, Owen found his tongue.

"That's insane."

"Is it?"

"Who the hell needs a Mate?"

"Your Mate is the other half of your soul." Lorde's own eyes, sapphire blue, glittered with sudden light. The Alpha's Dragon was reaching the end of its patience with his rebellion. "Are you seriously going to ask me who needs a whole soul?"

"Poetry," Owen snarled. "Nonsense. What happened to reclaiming the world?"

His Alpha's eyes lit as his own Dragon grew vexed with Owen's rebelliousness. "Jackson, what is a Dragon, truly?"

Wasn't it obvious? He rolled his eyes. "A warrior."

"Wrong. We're Protectors. We protect – Wellsprings, Mates, this world."

Details, details. Was 'warrior' really so different from 'protector'? "The best way to protect the world is to destroy those who seek to harm it. Namely, the Fangs of Apophis."

"And if the world dies while you defeat your foes? What good have you done?"

What a stupid question! The world wasn't in danger!

"Look, I know you want to fly off right this moment, breathing fire and laying waste to our enemies. But you can't. You're not ready."

"Why not?" Owen slammed his glass down, barely even noticing when its base cracked. "I was the one who destroyed that human trafficking ring in Amsterdam, remember? It was *me* who took care of those Rats smuggling drugs into Texas!"

Lorde's own eyes glowed now, blue sapphires. "You're not ready because you're not fully a Dragon."

Shock stunned Owen silent for one second, then his Dragon roared to life, burning with rage. Dagger-like claws sprouted from his hands, scales flashed along his arms as he grew, looming over his Alpha. "You insult me? You say I'm not a Dragon?"

Far from retreating, Lorde stepped closer. Their eyes locked and, even in the depths of its rage, his Dragon flinched as his Alpha faced him down. "A true Dragon is his own master. Look at yourself, Jackson. Look at yourself and tell me you're true."

The human half of his soul winced as the truth of that barb struck home. Yet, his Dragon raged. It longed to throw itself at Lorde. To challenge him, to fight him for the right to rule this Flight.

No, Owen ordered himself. *That isn't right.*

Slowly, ragged breaths shaking his frame, he ordered his Dragon back. It fought him every inch of the way, seething with fury at Lorde's 'disrespect.' But slowly, it subsided. Scales melted to skin once more. Fangs and talons vanished.

Lorde waited, ever-patient. In the end, when the last flame of rage died from Owen's eyes, his Alpha resumed.

"You think this is a physical battle. As if our enemies will line up on one side of a field, us on the other, and we'll lay into each other until only one of us remains.

"The battle we face is nothing like that. Our enemies are treacherous and sly. They won't fight us. They'll lurk in the shadows and poison our Wellspring. They'll seduce us with cheap pleasures, weaken our wills, tempt us into debauchery until we're no better than the Worms that lead them. This is a spiritual battle, a magical one. We need to prepare ourselves for it, not merely for combat."

"Fine," Owen grumbled. "You've made your point. I'll work on controlling my temper."

His Alpha wasn't letting him off the hook that easily. "That's your first chore – but you've got a lot more work before you're ready."

Another insult. By now, though, his Dragon did little more that snarl. "Fine. What else?"

Lorde fixed him with a stern, unflinching glare. "You fathered three children, yet you did not protect either them or their mother until I requested it."

Remorse pricked him as his leader's plot became clear. This wasn't something new. The Alpha had been watching him, testing him longer than he realized.

Trickery, his Dragon hissed inside his mind. *A trap.*

He felt its resentment, its injured pride. Hell, he shared those feelings. Yet, this accusation seemed to drive the Serpent near to hatred. The urge to challenge his Alpha, to 'avenge' his wounded pride, swelled within him. It was all Owen could do to contain himself.

And Lorde wasn't through with his accusations, either. "Over the years, you have engaged in numerous dalliances. You have not loved a single one of these women. The Wellspring has been awake for a full year now and you have not Claimed a Mate."

The force of his shame warred against his Dragon wrath, and slowly, slowly, it won. Owen turned away, unable to face Lorde's recriminations. They were true. What had he done over the years except entertain himself and dream of 'glorious' battles?

Seeing his submission, the sternness faded from the Alpha's face. "I do want you at my side. You are fearless in war. Yet, I need to know that your soul is pure and whole. I need to be sure I can trust you. That's why I'm sending you to California."

"I still don't understand how waiting on Witch Hares is going to help."

"Don't you?" A sly smile crept across Lorde's lips. "I'm sending you to a small town far away from the pleasures and distractions of the city. You'll take your children with you and you'll have plenty of time to become a true family. I'm also dumping you in the laps of thirteen beautiful young women. With any luck, one of those Hares will be your soul mate. If not, well, some Hares have a knack for fortune-telling. Perhaps one of them can point you in the right direction."

And, of course, it all made sense. Owen sighed, deeply depressed. His Alpha had a plan. He *always* had a plan.

Other Dragons would fly to war.

He was getting sent to the Time Out corner, to get his life in order.

"Do you accept your mission?"

'Mission.' That was ludicrous.

But what choice did he have? When your Alpha gave you an order, you obeyed.

Owen gave a sour nod.

CHAPTER 3

The third dinner in the Jackson household got off to a much better start.

Formal meals seemed completely alien to the Jackson children. They expected to gobble down a few bites out by the pool, in front of the tv, or wherever hunger hit them. Not that hunger ever bit them hard, given how much candy, snacks, and soda they devoured during the day.

Well, that was going to change. Time to bring rules and discipline to the Jackson household. Starting with family meals. The family that ate together, stayed together.

The first two dinners were complete disasters.

Tonight, Ariel was pleased to note, Trey and Brody did *not* come in covered in mud. They did *not* run straight out of the pool and plop down, sopping wet, on their cushioned seats. Trey still had leaves in his hair and a huge grass stain down the side of his face. Yet, in just three days, they'd made tremendous progress. Everyone showed up at 5:00 pm, with an appetite.

Except Sydnee.

"Sydnee?" Ariel prompted.

"What?" Curled in her chair at the end of the table, the girl didn't even glance up.

"What's the rule about cell phones at dinner?"

The girl rolled her eyes – a particularly annoying gesture. Ariel reminded herself that twelve was a tough age, especially for girls.

"Owen doesn't care if I use my phone."

Hearing a child use their father's first name grated on Ariel's nerves. When Mr. Jackson returned, she'd ask him about that. Some parents apparently liked it. For the time, she let the name slide.

"Dinner is a time for a family to be together. It's important that we be *here*, paying attention to each other. Not distracted by games."

"What-*ever*," Sydnee hissed. Thumbs darted across her phone, tapping out messages.

"Sydnee…"

"I'm saying goodbye, okay? Can I do that? Please? Or is that too much to ask?"

Sass and rudeness annoyed her. Yet, as Ariel opened her mouth to rebuke the girl, she saw something that killed her reproach.

Tears. Sydnee's eyes brimmed with them. Beneath all that bluster and attitude, she quivered on the edge of a meltdown.

Patience. Love and kindness will win the day eventually. Just remember that this is no ordinary family. You don't really know what these children have gone through.

So, unnatural as it was, she let the girl text away. When the cook brought out the salads, Sydnee did indeed put the phone away with a long, dramatic sigh.

"Who were you talking to?" the nanny asked, as if there had been no delay at all.

"A friend."

"From school?"

"No," Sydnee muttered. "I don't have any friends here."

The first piece of the puzzle fell into place. "So, you're chatting with your friends from New Jersey?"

A shrug. Sydnee speared a piece of lettuce with her fork and began to nibble on it.

"Having dinner at 5:00 pm must make it tough to talk to them." *That* got the girl's attention. Ariel looked into her startled eyes and pressed her advantage. "They're on the East Coast while you're on the West. They get out of school while you're still in. By the time you're home, they're eating dinner. You get an hour or so to catch up and then bam! It's *your* dinner time."

"Yeah. It sucks." Sydnee scowled at her plate, a tiny ball of misery.

"Hmm. Would it help if we moved dinner later? Say, to 7:00? We could have a snack at 4:00, which you could eat in your room. Then a light dinner later."

For once, Sydnee's eternal sulk melted away. "That would be cool." One tear escaped and trickled down her cheek before she swatted it away.

Ariel pretended she didn't notice, though her heart ached to see how much the girl missed her old life. She wasn't a bad child, she was lonely. Trey and Brody had each other to play with. Sydnee was alone.

"I'll talk to the cook about that. It shouldn't be a problem."

The girl didn't thank her. Yet, she did start eating her food with a bit more gusto.

I should talk to Mr. Jackson about excursions. He's wealthy enough that he might not mind if I took the children back East over Spring Vacation. I bet they didn't have time to say goodbye to anyone.

After salad, Mrs. Grover, the cook, brought out the main course. Ariel spent it gently encouraging the boys to use forks and napkins. The chicken disappeared. The vegetables… well, they lingered on both boys' plates. She pointed out that green beans were not poisonous. Trey and Brody picked at them then declared themselves full. Until dessert arrived and they miraculously rediscovered their appetites.

That was another thing to work on. One step at a time, however.

As the last bits of cake disappeared, a distinctive sound came through the open window.

…woppa woppa woppa woppa…

"HELICOPTER!" the boys shrieked in unison. They shot to their feet, shoving their chairs backwards.

"Trey! Brody!" Ariel growled before they could rocket off. At once, they popped back into their seats, twitching with eagerness. "What do you say before you leave the table?"

"Pleasemaywebeexcused?" It all came out in one breathless, mushed-together jumble of sound.

"You may be excused," she said. They cheered and sprinted off. It warmed her heart to know they were so anxious to see their father again.

"Sydnee, do you want to be excused too?"

"No."

How disappointing that, unlike her brothers, the girl didn't seem to care that Owen was home. Well, one step at a time. The cell phone discovery still felt like a huge breakthrough.

"Okay. Pardon me one moment, then."

Ariel rose and stepped over by the window where she could make sure the little boys stayed in the backyard. Watching the helicopter land was fine. Running out under those lethal blades was *not*.

Owen hopped out of the chopper and Ariel felt her heart skip a beat. His hair, unruly by nature, whipped about his chiseled features. He looked like an action hero, ready for boat chases in Venice or skiing away from Bad Guys in the Alps. Were all Dragons this stunning?

The excitement that coursed through her brought a flush to her cheeks.

That's no way to think about your employer, she scolded herself. *I should remember that he's 'Mr. Jackson' not 'Owen.'*

Mr. *Jackson* trotted across the lawn toward his sons. He waved... Trey and Brody waved back... then their father strode past them, leaving the kids to ogle what they really cared about.

The helicopter.

The sight made Ariel's stomach knot. So much for warm family reunions! Now, admittedly, he hadn't been gone long. But children and parents shouldn't ignore each other like that. Trey and Brody ought to run to their dad and he should scoop them into his arms. Like *her* parents had done!

There was something deeply wrong with this family.

She flicked away that doubt, like a Bear swatting a fly. There were problems? Fine. She'd solve them in time. After just three days, she and the boys were getting along wonderfully. And today, for the first time, she had an idea of what lay behind Sydnee's misery.

Their father? They'd bond in time too. Then she'd knit this family back together, the way it should have been from the start.

A door banged open. "George?" Owen... no, Mr. Jackson shouted as he strode into the room. "I've got news. Hey, Sydnee." The girl ignored him. "Hi, um... Mary?"

"Ariel," she corrected him. That stung a bit. Honestly, though, they'd only been together for three minutes. 'Mary' was at least in the ballpark.

The long-suffering George appeared in the doorway. "Yes, sir?"

"I'm turning Windhope Hall over to your competent hands."

George gave a small bow, neither worried nor surprised by this change. "You've been assigned elsewhere, sir?"

"Yup. Siskuh... mmm, Sisk-someplace, California. Middle of absolute nowhere, out in the woods. The Flight arranged a house for me."

"Staffed?"

"I assume so. Lorde told me to just take the kids and the nanny."

Sydnee froze and while her eyes remained glued on her last bit of cake, Ariel could see her listening closely.

"How long will sir be absent?"

"No idea. Could be three weeks. Could be seven years. Best bet is, don't expect us back any time soon."

A home in the country sounded wonderful to Ariel. No doubt, it would be nice (she couldn't imagine Owen living in a shack). And it *had* to be less intimidating than Windhope Hall!

Sydnee, however, exploded in rage. "You're joking! We're moving again?"

Owen shrugged. "Sorry, kid. Siska-whatever wasn't my first choice either, but that's where I got sent."

"So go already – but leave us here! Why should we have to go?"

Ariel drifted closer to the girl, frowning softly and trying to catch Sydnee's eye. She could understand her anger, yet this wasn't the proper way for a daughter to address her father.

"That's my orders. Me, kids, and nanny go."

"Why?" his daughter wailed.

The whine that threaded through the girl's voice made his eyes narrow. "My Alpha thinks I need to spend more time with my family."

That was good news! Ariel sent a silent blessing to Mr. Brandon Lorde, a man of uncommonly good sense.

Sydnee burst out in incredulous laughter. "Family? You think we're your family? Well, we're not! We're just the kids you got stuck with when Grampa died."

That crossed the line. "Sydnee!" Ariel took a step forward. "That is not true. Apologize to your father."

"No! It *is* true!" She leapt to her feet, snatched up her cell phone, and bolted for the stairs. "I hate you!" she shrieked as she ran out of the room. "You're *not* my father!"

The three adults watched her outburst, silent. As her footsteps faded away upstairs, Owen turned to Ariel. "How the hell did you get Sydnee wound up? She's the quiet one."

Her? He blamed *her* for this tantrum? That was idiotic! Yet, at the same time, a craven corner of her mind whispered that he might be right. This could be her fault. Everything *was*, right?

Ariel's eyes lit with outrage, both at him and her own willingness to accept blame. She was Bear Kin, not a dishrag! He had no right to treat her like this.

After a quick three-count, she slipped a leash on her flash of temper. "Your daughter is just lonely. She lost all of her friends when you brought her here. Now, after just one month, she's moving again. She knows she'll switch schools and have to start all over with new friends. Not easy to do, especially in a rural area where everyone knows each other." She herself had grown up in a small town and knew how unwelcoming children could be to strangers.

She expected him to bite her head off, given how badly he took it when George disagreed with him.

Instead, he pursed his lips. "Oh. I hadn't thought of that."

"That's why she's on her phone all the time. She's desperately trying to keep in touch with her old friends. Something the difference in time zones makes very difficult."

"Huh." The idea seemed as new to him as it had been to her. "Moving to… Siskel isn't going to help that either."

"Mr. Jackson," George interrupted. "If you have no further need of me…?"

"What? Oh, sure." At his employer's nod, the butler retreated from the room.

While Owen seemed open, Ariel pushed ahead with her plans. "Sydnee and I discussed this a bit over dinner. I've got some ideas about how we could help her."

"That would be awesome. I think I'm going to need a lot of help with this whole 'fatherhood' thing."

He looked at her, his green eyes unguarded. A soft, grateful smile stole across his lips. And, once more, Ariel felt her heart melt.

It wasn't his fault he was a haphazard father.

Well, it probably is…

He just needs a little help.

If he'll accept it…

Despite her doubts, she found herself beaming back at him.

He was so damned handsome when he was happy. How could she stay mad?

Sadly, she couldn't.

CHAPTER 4

$\mathcal{A}$riel woke into a dream.

Only a moment ago, she had lain down in her soft, quilted bed. Then she opened her eyes and found herself standing on a beach.

Spotless white sand curved away on both sides. Before her, waves rolled in from a crystal blue ocean, curling around her bare feet. Its waters mirrored the cloudless heavens, sky, and sea merging into one. Gulls circled overhead, crying plaintively.

A gauzy white gown wrapped around her, its cloth as delicate as tissue. It billowed in the wind, whispering across her bare skin. Ariel gaped at this strange garment, amazed, until the truth registered.

This is a dream, nothing more.

But it was so real! Salt tang laced the air. The sun blazed down, hot upon her skin. Could any dream be this vivid?

Behind her, cliffs ringed the beach, giving it complete privacy. An enormous blanket, red with gold lozenges, lay on the sand. And on it lay…

Him.

Owen Jackson. Sleeping.

Tanned, sleek, oiled… and almost naked. Taut muscles glistened in the sun, iron bands that ran in sharp definition along his legs. Her eyes rose hungrily along them, rising to his groin where a small blue sash hid his manhood from her. Nothing concealed his tight, sculpted abs, however, and the strong-jawed face she already knew and adored.

Watching him, she felt her body awaken. Warmth blossomed between her legs, echoing the sun's heat. Her breath grew shallow, rough, as she studied his elegance, the glorious, masculine perfection of his body.

Until the foolishness of it all struck her, and she laughed.

"Wow." Ariel forced herself to speak out loud just to break the illusion. "I'm dreaming about making love to my employer."

At the sound of her voice, Owen startled awake. "What the…" He bolted upright, sending his sash sliding lower. Not *quite* low enough to give her the glimpse she hungered for, though. "Ariel?"

His confusion unsettled her. This did *not* feel like a dream!

Joy lit his face and with a crow of delight, Owen leaped to his feet.

Now the sash *did* flutter to the ground. Ariel drew a sharp breath at the sight of his manhood. But the Dragon didn't even seem to notice his nakedness. Giddy with delight, he cried, "I did it!"

She had no idea what he was talking about. Absolutely nothing in this dream made sense. "Did what?"

"Found you!" His glee, the wonder in his eyes as he gazed at her made her head swim. "See, I didn't tell you everything about my assignment. My Alpha wants me to find my Mate. And I did: you!"

Ringing filled her ears and she wavered, dizzy. She was…
a Dragon's Mate?

"That's why we're sharing such an intense dream. This is
the Rite of Claiming, the ritual in which a Dragon Claims his
love and binds the two of them together for all time." He
laughed, shaking his head. "And here I thought it was going
to be tough to find my Mate. My Alpha made it sound like
the Quest for the Holy Grail!"

The Rite of Claiming. As the child of Shifters, Ariel had
dreamed about it when she was young. To be the soul mate
of a Dragon. To be Claimed by a lover born of passion and
fire, a protector created by Fate itself. To be promised a life
filled with adventure, wonder, magic, and love.

Ariel struggled to accept that as Owen babbled on.
"Remind me when I wake up that I need to strangle George
for buying you such dull, baggy clothes. I almost didn't
recognize you. It's like hiding a diamond in a shopping bag.
And your hair? In real life, do what you're doing here."

Her hand rose and she realized that her hair, unbound,
cascaded down her shoulders in golden waves.

"No more granny-buns." His words might have stung – if
not for the open hunger and adoration that lit his face.
"You're gorgeous, Ariel. Don't hide that, please. Not
anymore."

For a moment, she stood, rocked by a dozen emotions.
Wonder, that he could desire her. Longing for his body, hers
to Claim if she wished. And yes, pride. Pride that she, a mere
Kin, had been Claimed by a Dragon.

Then, in the midst of this most beautiful dream, a tiny
worm of doubt wriggled its way into her thoughts.

"Isn't there supposed to be a rite in the Rite of Claiming?"

His excitement dimmed too. "Yeah, my Dragon says
something and there's a cup and a dagger we, uh, do something with."

That was pretty vague. Ariel hoped the Dragon had fuller instructions. Both of them peered around the beach, yet found nothing except sea, sand, and blanket.

"I think you're supposed to have a cup," he told her. "Did you drop it someplace?"

"No, I didn't lose the sacred cup," she growled. Why did he always have to make everything someone else's fault?

Owen lifted the blanket. Nothing. He let it fall again and planted his hands on his hips. "Hello? Dragon?"

The azure sky overhead remained stubbornly empty.

She ought to help him search... but now that the shock had passed, she found she could only concentrate on one thing: the fact that he'd lost his little sash and was standing there, stark naked.

With taut muscles and lean lines, his buttocks were so different from her own soft, rounded curves. No body fat hid the tight lines of his flanks and their powerful muscles. He turned towards her, revealing everything. His cock, not yet aroused, lay long and thick against his thigh. Even as she watched, it stirred with the first touch of desire.

She shouldn't stare at him so! She *worked* for him!

Guilty, she stole a glance at his face. To her horror, she found him watching her. Enjoying the hunger, the yearning in her own body.

"Mr. Jackson, I'm so sorry..."

"Please. Don't call me that. It makes me feel ancient. We're going to be Mates, remember? I'm Owen. I'll always be Owen to you now, okay?"

'Owen'. With that one thrilling word, she felt the distance between them melt away.

He retrieved his little sash and wrapped it around his waist. Now he wore a belt that covered nothing. Frowning, he wound it around his privates but as soon as he let it go, it slipped off.

Ariel started to giggle. "Do you have any idea how this thing works?" he asked her.

"No, but you need to stop doing that," she waved at his latest effort, "or you're going to tie a bow around your, um…"

"Ah, to hell with it." He chucked the sash away with a rakish grin. "Why should I hide? You're clearly enjoying the view."

"Oh, I'm sorry, I shouldn't stare, I…" she stammered.

He stepped close. Only inches separated them. Any move, any gesture, and that tiny distance would vanish too. Ariel felt her body come alive, as if some primal, animal force swept over it. Fear made her heart race, fear that no man as hot, as gorgeous, could ever want *her*. That she, his nanny, had no right to want him.

Yet, as fear's cold claw touched her heart, a fire rose to defy it. A craving, a lust, hotter than any she had ever felt. It burned through her, its flames fanned by him, by that lean, male body. So close, so tempting. All she had to do was raise her hand and take what she wanted.

As her mind whirled, caught between desire and fear, her hand rose as if of its own will. It crossed that tiny space between them and softly, gently, touched his chest. She felt the heat of him, the hard power of his body, the beat of his own eager heart.

"It's all right." A faint glow lit his green eyes, the lightest brush of his Dragon's presence. "I love it when a woman looks at me like that."

All doubts, all hesitation, melted away. Tomorrow be damned. She wanted him, no matter what came of this. She ran her hand down his abs, reveling in their heat and steely lines.

Still, he didn't pull her close. Those inches separating them lingered, teasing. Ariel's breath grew ragged with anticipation and need.

His hand stroked her hair. That touch, the way her locks whispered across her own skin, made her shiver. Then his fingers traced their way along her cheek. They paused, lingering on her soft lips, before continuing their caress. At her shoulder, they found the knot that held her robe in place. One tug and it spilled to the ground in a shower of silk.

The ocean breeze, warm and damp, swirled across her skin. Touching her most secret places. She felt the sun's glow against her back, her buttocks. Her skin tingled at these new sensations and her body hungered for more.

Owen's eyes gleamed as he feasted on the sight of her intoxicating joy. "Shall we go for a swim?"

Ariel gave the blanket one longing glance before he caught her hand and drew her into the surf.

As soon as the first wave swirled around her calves, she forgot all about that blanket.

Sun baked water rose above her thighs. Sand, soft and yielding, nestled against her feet. Ariel gasped as the first wave lapped against her pussy, like some secret lover's tongue. Eyes closed, she tilted her head back and let the sun caress her face.

He led her onward, laughing. Deeper, they waded. Water reached her waist, her chest. In its embrace, she felt herself grow lighter. Her breasts rose, buoyed by the sea's embrace. Gentle waves washed across her nipples.

Owen stopped then and drew her close. Breasts teased and aroused by the water's play rubbed against his firm chest, drawing a sharp moan of pleasure from her. His cock, excited now, pressed against her thigh, eager and hard. Arms wrapped around her waist, lifting her from the ground. Held safe by the ocean's embrace and in her lover's strong arms, Ariel surrendered herself to passion.

He bent to kiss her. His lips, hungry, demanding, claimed

hers. With a sigh, her mouth parted, allowing his playful tongue to explore her.

Her hand, woven around his shoulders, glided down his back. Lean, smooth muscles flowed beneath her fingers. She stroked his flank, his thigh. Then her wandering hand found what it sought: the thick, hard shaft of his manhood.

Owen gasped with pleasure as her hand closed around him. Now it was his turn to lean back, eyes closed in ecstasy. His cock stiffened, swelled. Ariel stroked it, reveling in the speed of its arousal. Wetted by the ocean's waters, her hand glided across the tender skin of his balls. Owen moaned, his breath ragged with passion. Her strokes became firmer, faster, and his cock grew, nearly bursting with desire.

"Wait." Shuddering with longing, he caught her hand. He raised her fingers to his lips and kissed each one, sucking playfully at their tips. His iron-hard rod pressed against her crotch, driving her wild with its promise.

As the gentle waves swept around them, Owen crouched lower until his mouth joined the playful waters that teased her breasts. His shaft slid down her thigh, away from the cleft between her legs, drawing a quiet moan of denial from her. Then she felt the first kiss on her nipples and all other thoughts melted away.

Lips and mouth devoured her. His tongue circled her aureoles and flicked across the tips of her nipples. They stiffened, aching for him. The ocean joined them in their pleasure. Lifted by its gentle waves, her breasts pressed against him. Owen nuzzled them, showering them with kisses. He and the water lapped her skin, driving her nearly mad with longing.

Dipping down, his arms curled around her butt and lifted her from her feet. Ariel wrapped her long legs around his waist. Slowly, he lowered her. She felt the tip of his hard cock nuzzle against her pussy. Then its thick, hungry length slid into her. Ariel cried out as he filled her. Her legs squeezed tighter, driving him even deeper into herself, as her passion, her need, grew uncontrollable.

With hard, rhythmic thrusts, he took her. Each one sent waves of pleasure washing through her, driving her wild. Held aloft by the sea, she leaned back, floating in ecstasy. Weightless, she moaned, driven to frantic need by his unrelenting strokes.

With a cry, she came. Her legs clenched as pleasure took her, pulling her down hard upon his cock. That final stroke, and her cry of joy, drove him over the edge. She felt him explode within her, a glorious flash that mirrored the ocean's wetness.

Panting, they drew apart. Her legs, still trembling from pleasure, barely held her. Owen slipped an arm around her, and in his strong embrace, she walked back to shore where the blanket awaited them.

She wanted to tell him that she loved him. To confess that she adored him the first time she set eyes on him. To find words that could express how proud, how honored she felt to be Claimed by a Dragon.

Yet, she never got a chance. As they collapsed to the blanket, the dream beach melted away and she awoke in her own bed.

$\mathcal{S}$uccess!

The moment his eyes opened, Owen leaped out of bed and went sprinting down the hallway.

"Ariel!" He banged open her door.

With a yelp, his nanny awoke and scrambled back against the headboard. "Owen? M-m-mr. Jackson? What?" Her wide, shocked eyes met his for one second, then dropped to his waist. With her hair finally free, spilling down in unruly waves, she really did look like the woman of his dream. How could he have missed how gorgeous she was? He blamed George and those stupid potato-sack dresses he'd bought her.

"Tell me you dreamed last night!"

"I…" Her eyes wavered up to his once more, then quickly fell again. "Yes, I…"

"The two of us? The beach? Making love in the waves?"

"How did you… that really happened?" Her eyes grew wide with shock. And yet, they kept flickering downwards, as a blush crept across her cheeks.

What the hell was wrong with her? Owen looked down too – and immediately spotted the problem.

"You should put some pants on before the children see you," Ariel suggested.

Who wore pajamas, anyway? He plunked himself down on the bed and scooped her hands up. "Never mind the kids. Do you know what this means?"

"I…"

"You're my Mate!"

Tears welled up in her eyes. (Hopefully, they were tears of happiness, but you never knew with women.) "We're soul mates?"

"Yup!"

Ariel opened her mouth to say something else. Before she could, he gave her hands a quick kiss and bounded to his feet. "Hold that thought. I have to call my Alpha. I may not even have to go to Siskel!"

Back in his room, he grabbed his cell phone and a pair of pants.

Lorde answered on the second ring. "Jackson. Is there a problem?"

"No. Exact opposite. I got a Mate!"

"A Mate. On your first day of searching?"

Leave it to his Alpha to doubt him. "Yup. First day. It was the nanny you recommended." He wandered back down the hall towards her room. No doubt, Lorde would want to congratulate her.

At the moment, though, he seemed dubious. "Really? The nanny."

"Yup."

Ariel was sitting up now, a robe pulled close around herself. And, dammit, she was pulling her hair back into that stupid, boring bun she always wore. Why did she deliberately hide her beauty?

"I trust you know this 'nanny's' name?"

"Sure. Ariel."

"And her last name is…?"

Hmm. Good question. "Ariel, what's your last name."

"McDunnah." Her expression was pinched and guarded. Why the hell was *she* upset? He'd put pants on, like she wanted. He passed that name on to Lorde, who wasn't happy.

"So, you believe that you've Claimed a Mate, even though you don't know her name."

Well, he knew it *now*. Damn, there was no pleasing some people! "Yeah. It was one of those love at first sight kind of things."

Silence. "I see," Lorde said at last. "What did your Dragon have to say about this?"

Hmm. That actually was a bit strange. "I have to admit, it's been pretty quiet."

"Did it say anything during the 'Claiming'?"

Owen could hear the quotation marks around that word. "Well, no."

"Nothing?"

"No."

Ariel slipped over to her closet and pulled out a sweater three sizes too large. No, dammit! Not another one of those George specials! He tried to wave her away from it, but she wouldn't look at him.

"It didn't, perhaps, state that there was 'No Claim without truth'?"

"No."

His nanny pulled that sweater over her head and her slender, luscious form disappeared inside its boat-sized folds. Owen sighed.

Meanwhile, Lorde would *not* stop with the inquisition. "Describe the cup to me."

"Well… there wasn't one. It was… a lot more informal than I expected."

"Let me see if I understand you correctly," his Alpha said, his voice steely. "There was no cup, no dagger. Your Dragon gave no pronouncement. Did you at least allow her to look upon your soul?"

"No," he admitted. Ariel pulled on a pair of jeans stiffly, her back towards him. "But she's Bear-kin. Maybe my Dragon didn't think she needed to see it?"

"There was, in short, no 'rite' in your 'Rite' of Claiming." Now his voice wasn't just steel, it was ice cold steel. Steel buried under ten feet of Arctic ice. "What exactly makes you think you Claimed a Mate?"

"We shared a dream!" Owen protested. "What else could it be? She remembers it too! That's got to be the Rite, right?"

"Ask your Dragon."

"Fine."

Back me up, here!

Nothing.

Seriously? She's a fine Mate. She comes from some noble family or something. And she's beautiful! You saw her too. So speak up, and this will all work out great.

Despite his silent pleading, his Dragon did not give a peep.

"Well, Jackson?"

Owen's shoulders slumped in defeat. "It's not saying anything."

"Then you have *not* found your Mate," Lorde growled.

"But the dream…!"

"I have no idea what your dream was. Who knows, when magic returns fully, perhaps such shared dreams will become common. But there is one thing of which I am certain: this was not the Rite of Claiming. The union of two souls is unmistakable."

"But…!"

"Do you love her?"

That stopped him in his tracks. Certainly, the sex had been great… she seemed like a nice girl… there was no reason she wouldn't make a fine Mate… But as he stared at Ariel's back, at her hunched shoulders, the word 'love' stuck in his throat. He couldn't say it.

And Lorde knew exactly what his silence meant. "Go do your job, Jackson. And don't call me back until you can say that about a woman."

Click.

Dial tone.

Owen sighed and ran a hand through his hair.

Ariel waited, her back to him, staring into her closet.

"I'm sorry. My Alpha doesn't know what that dream was, but he doesn't think it was the Rite of Claiming."

"So, we're not Mates." There was something wrong with her voice; it sounded thick and choked.

"No. Sorry." And he truly was. He felt like an idiot and a cad.

"I'm not surprised," was all she said. Then she spun on her heels and brushed past him.

As she passed, he saw tears spilling uncontrollably down her burning cheeks.

He should say something, some apology that would make this easier for her.

Nothing came to mind, however. Words alone weren't going to clean up this mess. And so, he let her go, listening sadly as her footsteps echoed down the hall.

CHAPTER 6

*A*deline was a town of sharp divisions. Half of its people lived in single-wide trailers and prefab homes tucked in the woods. Half dwelled in multi-million dollar mansions perched on the hill tops. Each of these palaces boasted walls of glass, enormous windows that offered breath-taking views of Mt. Shasta. Screw the heating bills, these homes proclaimed. Money was no concern.

Owen's home fell in that latter category. A four-bedroom log 'cabin' with a Jacuzzi, a sauna, and a kitchen bigger than her old home in Louisiana. Staring out at the snow-covered mountain to the south, Ariel thought she'd never seen a place so lovely.

Owen wasn't as pleased. "I can't find the servants' rooms," he complained when he finished his circuit of the property.

It stung to be called a 'servant'... especially when, for one delirious moment, she had dared to dream she meant something more to him. But it *was* what she was, and she struggled to be more humble. "I could take a bedroom, if you don't mind me being near you and the children."

"Mind? What... oh! I didn't mean you!"

He looked genuinely shocked that she could think herself a 'servant'. Once again, her treacherous heart forgave him. Working for Owen gave her a constant case of whiplash. One moment, he said thoughtless, hurtful things. The next, he brimmed with apologies and kind gestures.

She wished he'd settle on one thing or the other. Clueless jerk or compassionate man. Bouncing between the two was killing her. Her heart ached all the time.

"I thought there'd be a maid and a cook, at least. Maybe a groundskeeper too."

"I can cook and clean." Caring for the house's expansive lawn and trees might be a bit much, but she'd find someone if necessary.

Owen didn't like her suggestion much. "That's not right. You're the nanny. You shouldn't have to clean and cook. Your job is to… to nan."

Jokes like that were why she found it so hard to think of him as 'Mr. Jackson.' "I can do all three."

"Really? And still watch the children?"

Quickly, she covered her mouth, trying to hide a grin. "Yes. Most parents do manage to feed *and* watch their children. And still clean."

"Huh." The sparkle in his eye showed that he saw how silly he was being. "Hadn't thought of that. I guess the world *would* be in trouble if people could only do one of those things."

She did laugh then, and he joined her.

Why couldn't every day be like this? He can be so gentle, so kind…

When he remembers that other people exist.

Time, she reminded herself. Time healed all wounds. Time would bring his family together.

The doorbell interrupted them.

Who could that be? The children were all on the back lawn, clearly visible. Puzzled, Ariel opened the door.

The woman standing on the doorstep could have walked straight out of *Vogue* magazine. Tall, leggy, with a Size 0 waist and the elegant face of an Arctic fox. Golden earrings dripping with diamonds and rubies sparkled in the waves of her raven-black hair. Her long white dress, woven of gossamer and silk, was some impossible designer dream that no one wore outside of a catwalk. A fox-fur stole curled around her shoulders.

The stranger smiled, her lipstick blood red. "I'm here to see Mr. Owen Jackson."

Just standing next to this vision made Ariel feel like a dumpling, and she fought a strong urge to fold her arms across her chest. Still, she forced herself to smile back. "Of course. Do come in. May I tell Mr. Jackson who's calling?"

"Clarissa Lange." The woman stepped inside, shrugged her stole off, and held it out negligently to Ariel. Like she was a coat hanger, not a human being. Gulping back her shame, she accepted it.

Owen stepped into the living room doorway, drawn by their voices. The newcomer's eyes widened. Ariel did *not* like the hungry, predatory glint that lit them as the woman eyed her employer up and down. "You *must* be Mr. Jackson."

"Owen, please."

Ariel didn't approve. He should have stuck with 'Mr. Jackson.' But no one asked her as she carried Clarissa's wrap to the closet.

"Owen, then," the woman purred. She held out her hand like some princess or 50's movie starlet.

Owen, ever gallant, promptly planted a kiss on it. Clarissa simpered. Ariel gritted her teeth and resisted the urge to dump the stole on the closet floor.

"Mr. Jackson?" She would remain formal, even if this other woman presumed. "This is Ms. Clarissa Lange."

"The Queen of the local Warren," Clarissa explained. "Mr. Lorde told me to expect you."

"Oh, right!"

She and Owen exchanged a few pleasantries as they drifted into the living room, with its grand mountain vista. Ariel drifted along behind them, forgotten.

Well, not entirely forgotten. As the Witch Hare sank gracefully to the sofa, she tossed Ariel a cool smile. "I'll have a glass of cabernet sauvignon."

Ariel bristled. Waiting on her family was one thing. Waiting on some arrogant stranger was *quite* another!

As if he sensed her outrage, Owen answered quickly. "I'm afraid we don't have any wines at all. We've only just arrived."

"Oh bother." The Hare's nose wrinkled. "I apologize if I've come too soon. I'm just so curious why we have such an illustrious guest."

Could she be any more of a boot-licker? Ariel felt a towering annoyance growing inside her. But, of course, Owen gobbled the false admiration up like a kid with an ice cream cone.

"My Alpha has sent me to aid your Warren in any way I can."

Clarissa's gaze flickered to Ariel then back to Owen. "Is there someplace we can speak privately? Without the servants?"

Now it wasn't even safe to talk around her? She turned away so that neither Shifter would see the indignation that lit her eyes. As calmly as she could manage, she said, "We haven't gotten the office set up yet, but I can go outside."

To her shock, Owen stood up for her. "There's no need.

Ariel is Kin. You can talk freely in front of her without giving away any Shifter secrets."

"You're sure she's trustworthy? One can't be too careful these days, what with the Fangs of Apophis so active."

"I trust her with my children," he replied, in a tone that wouldn't be contradicted. "Trusting her with my affairs is much less important."

Ariel wasn't sure he truly believed that (he often seemed to think that children took care of themselves naturally). Still, his defense warmed her heart and silenced the nasty Hare.

"As you will."

Owen Jackson, Ariel thought, *could be a damned charming man when he put his mind to it.*

She had half a notion to hover around in the doorway just to make the elegant woman uncomfortable. But that would be rude, and downright unprofessional. She also had work to do, like figuring out what dishes they had and what they needed. "I'll be in the kitchen if you want anything, sir."

"Thanks, Ariel."

When she retreated, however, she left the door open. *So she could hear any requests,* she told herself. Definitely *not* so that she could listen in on that Hare. She didn't trust Ms. Clarissa Lange one bit.

Most of the talk was a bit dull. Details on the Warren and its magical research – most of which flew over her head. Bears didn't work magic and she'd never known any Hares. Tons of compliments and flirting from Clarissa. Some of it so blatant and over-the-top that Ariel longed to fling a pot at her.

For the most part, Owen ignored it. Oh, he was flattered. Any man would be to have a beautiful, cultured woman fawn on him. Yet, there was a hint of reserve, of reticence, in his voice.

Maybe it was because Clarissa pumped him for information almost as blatantly as she flirted. What were his Flight's plans? Had Lorde gathered them all?

He shrugged most of it off, offering short, truthful, and uninformative answers. Yes, the Flight had been summoned. He didn't know what their plans were. All he knew was his own mission.

"To help us." Clarissa wrinkled her delicate nose. "I still can't imagine why we're so blessed. It's hardly like we're the only Warren around."

"My Alpha hopes you can give me some assistance."

"We'd be delighted, of course! How can *we* help?"

Owen squirmed and glanced up at the kitchen. His eyes locked with Ariel's. She turned away quickly, embarrassed to be caught listening. Not before she saw him wince and look away.

As if *he* was embarrassed.

What on earth could he think he'd done wrong? The fact that she wasn't good enough for his Dragon... well, that blame fell on her, not him.

"Are any of the Hares in town good with divination?"

"Passable, yes." Clarissa shrugged. "It's a difficult skill, however, and witches often specialize. What do you want to know?"

"Where to find a Mate."

Owen was so busy staring a hole into the floor that he didn't notice how those words hit his guest.

Ariel did. Shock and greed flared in the Hare's eyes before her polite mask dropped back into place. "So, the rumors are true. One of the Wellsprings has returned to life."

Why, oh why did Owen have to blurt that out! Ariel clamped a hand over her mouth to stifle a gasp.

He didn't even recognize his mistake. "Why would you say that?"

"The Dragons' Rite of Claiming is nearly mythic. Every Shifter has grown up with stories about it. And every one of us knows that the Rite vanished when the Wellsprings died."

"Oh." Owen winced.

"Can you tell me where it is? How healthy it seems?"

"No." He shook his head – never realizing that, once again, he confirmed that a living Wellspring existed.

"I understand completely," Clarissa assured him. "And I would be delighted to introduce you to all the young Hares in my Warren. Any one of them would be honored to be Claimed."

"Thanks." Stiff and unmoving, he didn't seem pleased by that prospect. A fact that lightened Ariel's mood.

But only for a moment, because the Hare continued. "You're also in luck. 'To Find True Love' is one of the oldest, most traditional spells we know. I should be able to help you, if no one in my Warren suits."

Unable to bear the pendulum swings of her heart, Ariel drifted to the back of the kitchen and slipped outside through the side door.

Why did this hurt so much? Real though it felt, the dream they shared was nothing. Not the Rite of Claiming. Not a pledge of true love. It was a pleasant dalliance, nothing more.

She wasn't Owen's Mate.

She had to accept that, and move on.

And she had to allow him to move on too, because his Alpha was right: Owen needed to be whole. He needed, and deserved, true love.

Even if that love wasn't her.

Her petty jealousy didn't help either of them. Yet, jealousy's sting was less painful than the alternative.

Grief. For her shattered dream. For her lost hope. For a bright future that was tarnished so soon after it began.

Ariel sat down on the kitchen steps as the first tear fell.

CHAPTER 7

As the cool days of May slipped past and June's berry-filled heat arrived, Owen found the town of Adeline growing on him.

The people were friendly and welcoming, a nice mix of wealthy summer people and down to earth loggers and farmers who stayed year round. Despite its tiny size, it boasted one 'fancy' restaurant, a little French place that only seated eight customers. The food was far below the level of Los Angeles or New York City. Yet, the chef knew him now and treated him like family whenever he ate there. That hospitality, that familiarity, gave dinners out a savor he'd never found in any Michelin rated meal.

He ate there a lot. Three times a week.

With a different woman each time…

True to his mission, he took each member of the Adeline Warren on a date. Every Friday, Saturday, and Sunday night, he escorted a different Witch Hare to "Chez Moi." Every night after dinner, he took them home – and never gave them a second thought.

The chef laughed and called him a 'player'. His wife, the sole waitress, gave him stink eye. Honestly, though, it was...

Dull.

The same small talk, night after night after night.

Oh, the girls were fine. Every one of them was pretty and polite. A couple of them were *seriously* into this magic stuff and prattled endless about the Warren's work. Which was about as much fun as listening to a nuclear physicist drone on about atomic structure for two hours. Most, however, tried to hold actual conversations. Still, he had little in common with them.

His Dragon maintained a stony silence throughout all of his dates. Some days, Owen wondered if his Shifter soul had fallen asleep or died of boredom.

Outside the dinners, he didn't have a lot of work. Visit the Warren... listen to updates on the area's 'chi' and 'mana' and 'Feng Shui'... understand *none* of that... smile politely. Rinse and repeat, day in and day out. Fortunately, that stuff only took a couple hours. Then he headed home.

When they arrived, 'heading home' just meant 'go back to the house and be bored there instead of being bored at the Warren.' But after only one day of that, Ariel lent a hand. She suggested chores. Help the boys build a bug terrarium. Take the boys swimming while she and Sydnee went to Mt. Shasta to get a 'mani-pedi' (whatever the hell that was...).

To his shock, the kids turned out to be... fun.

They noticed things he never saw. Lightning bugs and spiders. A pile of branches a boy could crawl under and make a fort out of. A tree that absolutely, positively, *had* to be climbed. Sydnee remained aloof and confusing, but Trey and Brody barreled into the world each morning brimming with excitement. Owen found he loved that, loved joining in their adventures.

One afternoon, as he drove up the driveway, they scrambled out to meet him. There was a 'gigantous' frog in the pond! He had to see it, now! The boys dragged him out there, one tugging on each hand. No rest until they'd shared this wonder with him.

With *him*.

They wanted *him* to be part of their little lives.

On that day, Owen felt the first stirrings of something. Some deep, gentle emotion he'd never felt.

Trey and Brody weren't just children; weak, tiny creatures that needed protection. They were *his* children. He found himself thinking of them – Ariel, Sydnee, the boys – throughout the day. Looking forward to his time with them. Feeling delight when they shared their own lives with him.

Was this love? Was this why his Alpha had sent him here?

If so… He hated to admit it, but Lorde was right.

He could feel the effect on his Dragon. For years, it had slumbered, rousing only when he called upon it in battle. As soon as their foes were vanquished, however, it slipped back into torpor. Honestly, most days, he felt more like a man than a Dragon.

Maybe Lorde was right. Maybe that was a bad, bad thing…

Well, his Dragon was awake now!

Owen treaded water in the deep end of the pool as Trey and Brody fought to achieve the biggest cannonball 'ever'. There wasn't an enemy for miles – and yet, he could feel his Dragon. Ready. Watchful. It noticed when the boys ran too quickly or rough-housed on the cement walk. It always knew where Sydnee lay, sunning and sadly reading her phone. Nothing was wrong. Yet, he knew that, if a crisis arose, that great serpent would not be caught unawares.

It watched. It protected.

And, for the first time in years, Owen felt alive.

He felt like a *Dragon*.

Movement over by the house caught his eye. Ariel emerged carrying a pitcher of a pale, pinkish liquid. 'Agua fresca' she called it. Water and sweet berries – the nectar that she had successfully used to wean the kids off soda.

Her hair, freed now, fell to her shoulders. Under the summer sun it burned gold, a glorious crown that refused to be ignored. And her shopping trips with Sydnee had done wonders for her. Turned out, his daughter had *much* better taste than his butler. Ariel didn't wear fancy clothes often; that wasn't her style. But with Sydnee's encouragement, she'd transformed. Gone were the lumpy sweaters and baggy jeans that George dumped on her. Now, her slacks flattered her long, shapely legs instead of hiding them. Her flowing peasant blouse fluttered in the wind, pulling tight against the curves of her breast.

Ahem. He'd better stop looking at her like that or he'd have to wrap a blanket around his waist.

Ariel set the drinks down on a table. Would miracles never cease? Sydnee put down her cell phone (voluntarily!) and scrambled over to help her. And she smiled. Smiled!

Owen found himself grinning foolishly. This was heaven. The five of them, together. Just like a family.

A poor choice of words. As soon as he thought it, his joy faded.

Because they weren't a family. They were a Dragon, his children, and the nanny. His Dragon's total silence confirmed his worst fears: no matter how deliriously hot their shared dream might be, it wasn't the Rite of Claiming.

"Snack time!"

The boys cheered and power-walked (no running near the pool!) to get their drinks. Owen swam to the edge and pulled himself out.

Surrounded by his children, Ariel glowed with joy. She was what made this family. She was the one who found ways to involve him in the boys' games in those early days. It was she who lured Sydnee into the kitchen and got the girl to tell her about the food her grandfather had made for the kids. Together, the two of them recreated those simple, hearty meals. Bringing a touch of home and happiness back into dinner.

Ariel was the soul of this family. The joy that brought it to life.

Yet, she was also the dagger in his heart.

He needed a Mate. And it wouldn't be her.

Irritably, Owen whipped a towel around himself. *Say something!* he ordered his Dragon. *Speak up! If you Claim her, everything will be perfect. I'll complete my mission, I'll have a family. All it takes is one word from you.*

His Shifter soul didn't deign to respond. It scanned the skies, the woods, alert for danger.

It ignored all his pleas, no matter how desperate.

Ariel held out a glass to him as he walked over. Did her eyes linger on his bare chest? Her fingers brushed his as she passed him his drink. Did they stay, touching, for one tender moment?

God, he was cruel. Owen winced and turned away.

He had raised her hopes to the sky – and then shattered them. Now, she lived here. Close to him, yet never touching. Caring for his children, yet never their mother. Forced to watch while he spent his days searching for the woman to replace her.

Those words hurt. They dripped venom into his heart.

But they were true.

If he found a Mate, Ariel would need to leave.

No woman would tolerate his nanny in her home. The children adored her. And he... he felt something for her. There was an energy between them, a desire that threatened to break free every time he saw her.

No woman would accept a rival in her own home. When he Claimed a Mate, he would have to send Ariel away.

Or you could Claim her already! he snapped at his Dragon.

It stirred, annoyed by his persistence. A deep bass growl, more thunder than voice, rumbled in his head.

Do you love her?

Well, sure. Probably. Not that he had any experience in that, of course. Even if it wasn't love, it was a damned intense emotion. A yearning like nothing he'd ever felt.

His Dragon turned its mind elsewhere, leaving him to stew.

Why was it so hard to accept that word?

Love.

"Owen?"

With a guilty start, he dropped those dark thoughts.

Surrounded by chattering kids, Ariel watched him. "Is everything okay? You seem distracted."

"Yeah." His smile seemed to reassure her. Even if it was false. "Everything's fine."

But it wasn't.

It wasn't at all.

CHAPTER 8

*A*s the clock hands swept toward noon, Ariel found herself worrying.

Owen was late.

Normally, trips to the Warren took a couple hours. By 10:30 am the rumble of his Jeep announced his return home. She made lunch in the bright, airy kitchen, serenaded by the family's laughter as they played outside. Those timeless moments held enough joy to break her heart.

Eleven o'clock came and went, and still, no sign of Owen. Something must have happened at the Warren. Maybe the Hares finally found some work for him to do.

Or maybe he finally found his Mate.

Her heart skipped a beat. A cloud scudded in front of the sun, throwing the kitchen into gloom, as if the sky could feel her fear.

It never left her. It the midst of her joy, in the heart of this family, that fear lurked. One day, probably soon, Owen Jackson would find the woman who would complete him. He would Claim her, uniting them forever.

And what would happen to her then? He'd have to fire her.

If he didn't, she'd leave. To see him in love with someone else… it would kill her.

No, there was no question. The day he found his Mate was the day she had to leave.

And every morning, she wondered if this day was *the* day.

A distant shriek jerked her out of her sorrow.

Ariel snapped to attention, immediately scanning out the window for the children.

The boys were still playing with their trucks on the back lawn. Good. But Sydnee was no longer with them, obsessing over her phone.

Cursing her moment of inattention, Ariel strode outside.

There she was! Sydnee pelted across the lawn toward home.

Ariel sprinted toward her. Nobody who was seriously hurt could run that fast, but the girl was clearly frightened.

She caught the child as she staggered up. "Sydnee! What's wrong? What happened?"

"There's a girl! In the woods!"

That took the edge off her fear. Strange neighbors weren't a threat. Plus, a quick scan of her charge revealed no injuries. Not even a bruise.

"And a man! I think he grabbed her or something."

Ariel's eyes narrowed and a Bear's fierce love rose inside her. Strange men lurking in the woods was quite another matter. Yet, she couldn't see any movement in the woods. "Where? Show me."

Nervous, Sydnee led her to the edge of the lawn. "She was right here. She wouldn't come out, but she talked to me. Her name's Tamar."

What an odd name. Was it from the Bible? "And the man?"

"I don't know. Tamar said she was hungry so I went to get her some food. When I came back, I heard her cry and… and I saw a man. Here."

"What did he look like?" Ariel edged forward, keeping herself between Sydnee and any hidden strangers.

"Nasty! He was dirty and skinny and… and… nasty! Just nasty!"

She pushed her way through a bit of undergrowth – and immediately came onto a path. Broad, worn flat by countless feet, it was clearly some local trail. Probably ran to the town or high school.

But where did it come from?

"Is she there?" Sydnee called.

Ariel glanced up and down the wide path. "No, I don't see anyone."

"I'm not lying!"

"I know you're not," Ariel assured her. Uneasy, she returned to her own property. "What did Tamar look like? Did she look okay?"

"No! She was filthy and skinny and she said she was starving. And her clothes were awful. Way too small and patched and dirty."

All kinds of warning bells went off in her head. "Was she hurt?"

"I don't think so."

"Did she say anything odd?"

"Like what? I mean, she said she wasn't supposed to talk to strangers."

That wasn't odd, that was sound advice.

"I think he hurt her!" Sydnee whimpered. "She cried."

Real danger – or an overprotective parent? "Did you see which way the man went?"

"That way." The girl pointed down the trail, deeper into the woods.

"Ariel?" By now, the commotion had drawn the boys. They inched close, dump trucks clutched to their chests. "What's wrong?"

"Oh, nothing." Was that a lie or not? Was there a child in danger here? Or had Sydnee simply been startled by an ugly, poor man?

She didn't know.

But, being Bear-kin, she couldn't live with not knowing. "Sydnee, I need you to do something for me, okay?"

Wide-eyed, the girl nodded.

"Take your brothers back inside the house. Lock the doors. Don't open them for anyone unless it's your dad or me. Understand?"

All of the children paled. "What are you going to do?" Sydnee whispered.

"Nothing to worry about." She forced a cheery smile even though her heart beat fast. "I'm going to see if I can find Tamar or that man."

"But..."

"I'll be fine. Now, go."

"Shouldn't we call the police?"

"We're not sure anything's wrong. That man could be Tamar's father." Or the strange child could be in danger, right now. Ariel didn't want to mention it, but in rural areas, it could take up to a half hour for the police to arrive.

She couldn't wait that long. If Tamar really was in trouble, she needed to act. Now.

Once the children were safe inside, Ariel headed down the path at a jog. It wound through the pine trees, crossed a small creek on an ancient plank bridge, and ran along the base of the nearby hills. Soon, she came to a fork. One branch – clear, broad, and well-used – continued along the lowlands. A fainter path split from it and cut directly up the hillside.

Ariel considered the two routes. A lot of people traveled the big one, which meant the odds were good that Tamar went that way. But if you were up to no good, you wouldn't go where everyone else was.

She chose the small path.

After a few hundred yards, she began to regret her choice. The path faded to a shadow of a trail that switched back and forth across the hard packed earth of the hillside. She began to wonder if she'd stumbled on a deer trail, something human feet weren't meant to walk.

Yet, when she reached the crest of the ridge, she came out on a small pond. Here, the track grew clearer. It led to a rutted dirt road, and the road led to a small clearing.

It was, as Sydnee would have said, 'nasty'.

Six rusting cars lay scattered about, surrounded by other debris. Metal barrels, a cracked toilet, dozens of bald tires. Ariel stepped carefully. The last thing she needed was a trip for a tetanus shot. In the midst of the squalor stood a decrepit trailer. Moss grew thick on its sagging roof. Did people actually live in that thing? She wouldn't put chickens in it, much less herself!

A man sat on an upturned bucket in front of the trailer. One glance, and Ariel agreed with Sydnee's assessment: nasty. Beady eyes glowered out of a small, pinched face. Oily locks of brown hair lay plastered to his skull. His patched jeans and wife-beater t-shirt were covered with grease, food, and other mysterious, vile things. Beyond the dirt and squalor, however, there was something alarming about him. The way his shifty eyes roved, never stopping. His hunched, unfriendly posture. She couldn't put her finger on the source, but her gut warned her this man couldn't be trusted.

Still, good manners were never wrong. "Hello, I'm Ariel Mc…"

He spat, shocking her into silence. "This is private property. Yer trespassing."

All right. So much for etiquette. She folded her arms across her chest and planted her feet. "Were you down at our house a few minutes ago?"

"I didn't git on your land and I'll thank you to git off mine. Now."

"You were spying on my children." Technically, they weren't 'hers.' But they felt that way.

"I seen 'em," he admitted, "as I walked by. On a public path."

"I don't want you watching my children!"

He bared yellow, stained teeth in a snarl. "Keep 'em inside if you don't want nobody seeing 'em. Ain't my fault I could see 'em from the trail."

Ariel surveyed the junkyard around her. "Where's the girl?"

"What girl?"

"Tamar."

He gave no sign that the name meant anything to him. "Don't know no 'Tamar'."

"Is she your daughter?" Lord, she hoped not! The thought of a child living in this filth set her Bear-blood boiling.

The stranger laughed at that suggestion. "Daughter? Do I look like the kinda man a woman would sleep with?"

Honestly, no. Which made this all the more worrisome. "Sydnee, my... my little girl..." She choked back the phrase that wanted to slip free: 'my daughter.' "She said you did something to a girl she was talking to."

"Oh, is that yer 'Tamar'? Yeah," he shrugged. "When I come by on the path, there was a girl in the woods."

"Sydnee says she heard her scream."

"Yep. Guess she didn't hear me come up." He gave her a

broad grin that was a few teeth short of a full smile. "You'd scream too if you turned around and saw me."

Well, yes. She might. The first fingers of doubt touched her.

"She took off running. Dunno why. Dunno her, dunno where she went. I'd check down the main trail if I was you."

"Do you mind if I look around for her?"

"Hell yeah I mind." Real anger lit his small eyes. "I don't barge into yer house and look about."

One flash of fury, and then that anger sank into sullen petulance. "Course I mind it less 'n' I mind you calling the cops, so go ahead and have your look."

That didn't sound like an innocent man! "What makes you think I'm going to call the police?"

"You look like the sort that does that to people. Calls the cops, bitching about permits 'n' zoning 'n' all sorts of other shit."

"And you're worried about that?" she sniffed.

He waved at the yard around him. "Woman, I got six trucks here. You see a registration sticker on any one of them? I ain't done nothing wrong but that ain't gonna stop the cops from making my life miserable. Cost me a fortune in fines and fees and whatnot. So go on." He spat again, a yellow glob of phlegm. "Snoop all you want. I don't give a shit."

He was worried about lapsed registration? That *did* sound innocent to her, and Ariel had to wonder if she was jumping to conclusions.

And yet…

And yet, there was something *wrong* about this man. Something shifty, sly, and untrustworthy. She couldn't ignore her instincts.

Not when a child could be in danger.

And so, she searched the property. Inside junked cars and

an abandoned refrigerator which really ought to be chained shut. Around a shack and the remains of an ancient chicken coop, long since abandoned by its flock. She even stuck her head inside his trailer (which turned out to be the cleanest place on the property, much to her surprise).

All her efforts turned up nothing. No Tamar. No signs of a struggle or a pen where a kidnapped child might be locked away. No toys, no children's clothes… not a single scrap of evidence against him.

All the time, he watched her, glowering silently. Finally, she had to give up.

"You done?"

"I am." She ought to feel embarrassed by her rudeness, yet she couldn't shake the feeling that she had missed something. "Thank you."

"You ain't welcome. Will you just git now?"

"I will." Before she left, though, she had one more question. "What's your name?"

"Smith. Walker Smith."

Good. A very unusual name. One that would show up easily in Google searches. Ariel nodded and headed back toward the path home.

You haven't heard the last of me, Mr. Smith. You're up to something, and I'm going to find out what it is.

CHAPTER 9

Another day at the Warren. Another whole lot of nothing to do.

Owen had the patter down now, after a month of daily visits to the spacious farmhouse that held Clarissa and her Witch Hares. Every morning, he did his round of the researchers. Same questions, same answers.

"Morning, Elisi! Need anything? Nope? Okay. Hey, Gerta, how's the research going? Great, great, any angles I can help with? No? Okay. Hello, Sandy. Feng Shui still looking good this morning? Yup? Great, great, uh, you need anything? No? Okay..."

Last stop on the tour was Clarissa Lange's office. As always, the Witch Queen was a vision. Perfect curls, flawless makeup, the hint of a rich perfume – Chanel? Hermes? – lingering in the air around her. "I'm starting to feel guilty about making you drive over here. Can I at least get you something to drink? Wine? Whiskey?"

At eight in the morning? Even at his worst, he never started drinking this early. "No thanks. If there's nothing you need, I'll just head home." A full day with the kids and Ariel actually sounded wonderful. Maybe they could head over to Mt. Shasta. Have lunch at some nice little bistro, go for a hike.

Or, better yet, find someplace to park the kids for a bit so that he and his nanny could have some time alone. They got so little of it. Who knew that children were so much work?

Well, parents probably know that.

True – but it was news to him.

Clarissa wasn't letting him go so easily, however. "No, please, sit. Let's talk a bit, shall we? Maybe I can take you out for lunch."

It was *eight*. Did she expect him to sit around, twiddling his thumbs, for four hours?

Vexed, his Dragon stirred. He wasn't a lapdog. He was a Dragon. Helping a Warren was fine (sort of… though the task felt menial…). But why wouldn't Lorde let him check in by phone, rather than in person? Why ask him to waste all this time?

He probably expects me to get to know these ladies. See if one of them might be my Mate.

When what he really wanted to do was go home to her.

Ariel.

The one woman who, he knew, definitely wasn't his Mate.

That thought took the wind out of his Dragon, and it settled again, grumbling. Owen, too, took a seat.

Clarissa's bright smile widened. "You forgot this yesterday, by the way." She stepped over beside him and held out a tiny vial.

Oh, right. Morning dew, collected when the first ray of sunlight hit it, by a naked virgin.

According to the Hares, this was a fantastic way to spot your True Love. Wash your face with it in the evening and it would bring you dreams of your soul mate.

Elisi finished the potion three days ago. And, for three days, he'd left it behind. "Sorry."

"I'm starting to think you don't want help finding a Mate. Is there someone who's caught your eye?" Her hand dropped to his shoulder and lingered there.

"Not really, no. Sorry. I guess Dragons are pretty fussy."

"And why shouldn't they be?" Her voice grew deeper, sultrier. One finger brushed against his ear. "Dragons are the kings of our world. Royal, regal. Dominant. The lords, by nature, of all Shifter kind. You deserve the most beautiful, most powerful Mate. No lesser woman is worthy of you."

She stroked his neck lightly.

Just in case I'm a complete moron and can't see what she's hinting at...

Owen stood, breaking the contact, and wandered over to the window. "I don't think power has much to do with it. My Alpha Claimed a normal woman. Well, she's Kin, but nobody knows where the Shifter blood came into her family."

"Interesting." The Witch Hare followed him. The scent of her perfume surrounded him and then she snuggled up against him. "What's her name?"

"Hannah."

"Hannah what?"

"I don't recall her maiden name."

"Ah." Clarissa sounded oddly disappointed by that.

"You could ask my Alpha."

"Oh, it's not really important." She set the vial of dew on the sill in front of him.

Owen ignored it. He tried to ignore her, too, though she was making that difficult.

"Have you seen the Wellspring?"

"No. Lorde doesn't let many people go there. Trying to keep it secret as long as possible. It's easier to defend a place if your enemies don't know where it is."

She laughed, a rich, throaty chuckle and pressed against his side. "Clever. Though, I'd guess it's somewhere near Los Angeles, judging by how much time Mr. Lorde spends there."

She tracked his Alpha's movement that closely? The admission disturbed him – until he remembered that she *was* working on Wellsprings. They probably spoke on a regular basis. Nothing ominous there.

And hell, she was dead, flat wrong. The Wellspring was in Upstate New York. He knew that, even if he'd never been there.

"Does your Flight have any idea why this Wellspring survived when all the others faded?" Clarissa asked.

"It was dead too."

The Witch Hare wrinkled her nose. "I doubt that."

Owen shrugged. "My Alpha says his Mate woke it."

"How? She's not a Witch Hare or even a Shifter!"

"Love."

Clarissa gave a very unladylike snort. "Nonsense. Despite the fairy tales, love doesn't have any magical powers."

"If you want details, you'll have to ask him. He insists the love of his Mate brought it to life."

"You realize that that's ridiculous, yes? An oxymoron on its face. Dragons need Wellsprings to Claim their Mates. Ergo Lorde's Mate couldn't have awoken it, because she wouldn't have *been* his Mate unless it was already awake."

"Like I said, I don't know all the details. I guess it was partially awake when they met."

"Because of her? Because she's such a 'loving' person?" The Hare's lip curled.

"Mmhmm." Owen wasn't going to argue. Let her believe what she wanted.

Out of the blue, Clarissa suddenly asked, "Would you like to see our Wellspring?"

The offer surprised him – and intrigued him too. In all these weeks, he'd never been shown the site.

"Sure."

"Follow me, then."

Off to one side of the farmhouse, a small road, graveled with white stones, cut into the woods.

No one's trying to hide this *Wellspring, clearly!*

To be fair, though, this one was dead. Literally, scores of dormant Wellspring lay scattered across the globe. Nothing special about the Adeline spring, except that it was being studied.

"I warn you, you're going to be disappointed. If you're not sensitive to magic, there's not much to see. But I can explain our research to you."

To his relief, once they entered the woods, Clarissa stopped draping herself over him. She stuck close to one side of the path, letting him put a good couple of feet between them.

Soon, the little lane opened onto a tiny glade. Owen saw a low stone border – the remains of a well house? – and a wrought iron bench…

…then something shifted under his foot.

Click…

Reflexes kicked in, both draconic and human. Owen spun, shielding Clarissa. Even as he did, his Dragon was in full attack. Talons, claws, scales rippled across his body.

BOOM!

The ground exploded.

Gravel sprayed like shrapnel around them. It tore through his pants and shirt. If Owen had been just a man, it would have flayed the skin from his bones. Fortunately, he was a Dragon. Even in his fully human form, the Great Serpent cast its shadow on him. Rocks bounced off his body as if from plate armor. Clarissa wasn't as lucky. The Witch

Hare screamed in terror as stones sang through the air around her. Yet, thanks to his honed, protective instincts, most slammed into him, not her.

A quick scan revealed no enemies. Owen spun toward the fragile woman. "Are you all right?"

"What was that?" A thin trickle of blood dribbled down the Hare's face.

"Land mine. Small one."

"What?"

Had the blast deafened her? "Anti-personnel land mine," he repeated.

"What?" She blinked… blinked again… and suddenly, her eyes rolled back in her head and she crumbled.

With a curse, Owen caught her before she hit the ground.

No time to look for clues now. He scooped the unconscious Hare into his arms and sprinted back to the Warren.

An hour later, after he completed a full survey of the property, he returned to find Clarissa in bed, surrounded by doting Witch Hares.

"How do you feel?" he asked as he pulled a seat close to her. He wore what could, politely, be called a 'toga'. No Witch Hare was even close to his size and he'd been forced to search the property with a sheet wrapped around himself.

"Bruised, but I'll survive. Thanks to you." She gave his hand a grateful squeeze.

"It was nothing."

"Nothing?" A fluttery, weak laugh escaped her. "You saved my life. I am in your debt. *Forever.*"

That last word was weirdly somber. Like she meant it as some sacred pledge. Her intensity, her painful earnestness, made him strangely uncomfortable.

"It's my job." He pulled his hand free and leaned back just

out of reach. "I'm glad I was there to protect you. Though, I have to say, it was a surprisingly weak charge."

Around him, the Hares startled. "Weak to a Dragon, perhaps," Clarissa scoffed, "but it would have killed one of us."

"It might have. Elisi, you need to make sure that everyone stays inside this afternoon."

"Are there more?" Clarissa's assistant shivered.

"Yes." His voice grew grim. "Two more near the Wellspring. One over by the barn." Murmurs of horror met his words. "Luckily, they're metal, not plastic. I'm heading to Shasta now to get a metal detector. I want everyone to remain here, where it's safe, until I've checked the grounds thoroughly."

"Who would do this?" Elisi whispered.

But they all knew the answer to that. "The Fangs of Apophis."

Normally, that announcement would have made his heart sing. If the Fangs were here, battle wasn't far away. And nothing made him feel alive like a fight.

Yet, now Owen felt himself seethe with anger. If battle wasn't far away then it was too damned close to his family. For the first time, he felt the weight of his protective duties. Battle wasn't just an opportunity for glory and fame. It was a risk, a danger to those he loved.

He would find their enemies and stop them. That prospect had always set his soul soaring with fierce glee. Today, unlike every other time, it filled him with a sober determination, not delight.

"Look, here's what I know so far. These devices are relatively weak. They would kill or maim a Hare, but most Shifters would survive the blast. The Fangs could have planted something much larger, something that could take out a Wolf or a Bear. But they didn't."

Clarissa waved away his concerns. "They probably didn't expect any warriors. This is a Warren, after all. Though, that does mean that they don't know you're here."

"Maybe, but here's the really odd part. They're shaped charges, not indiscriminate weapons. Like they want to kill one person, not lots."

"So you're saying that someone is trying to assassinate me?" The queen's eyes grew wide.

"Or me," Elisi added. "As chief researcher, I visit the Wellspring site every day."

"I don't know." Owen rose to his feet. "Maybe I can find more clues this afternoon. After I get that detector."

"Wait." Clarissa caught his hand as he turned and, with a surprisingly strong grip, pulled him down onto the bed. "I have seen strange people in town. Ugly ones. They may have been Rats. I couldn't get close enough to tell."

Rats. Owen's nose wrinkled. The most loathsome Shifters. Spies, assassins, poisoners – and servants of the Fangs. "I'll watch for them. Thank you for the warning."

She leaned in, her musky perfume still strong, despite the day's mishaps. Her lips, warm and soft, met his.

Startled, Owen jerked back.

Clarissa ignored his surprise. "Thank you," she murmured, her voice low and husky. "I hope, someday, I can repay you for saving my life."

He retreated then, before she could spell out exactly how she planned to do that.

CHAPTER 10

By the time Owen made it home, the sun had set. Ariel waited for him, reading a book. When he came through the door in his make-shift toga, she burst into giggles.

"What happened to your pants?"

"They were blown up by a land mine."

Her laughter lasted for one more second – until she realized he was serious. Then she sprang to her feet and darted over. "Are you all right?"

"I'm fine. The pants didn't survive, though."

She caught his hands and scanned his face, anxiously searching for any sign of a lie.

The worry in her eyes raised odd, protective urges in his heart. What would it be like to come home to this, every night? To a woman, to a family, that cared for him?

"Seriously, I'm okay. It takes a lot more than a weak land mine to hurt a Dragon."

"There's such a thing as a 'weak' land mine?"

"These ones were strange." Reluctantly, he pulled free of her gentle grip. "Let me get out of this sheet and I'll explain.

Then we need to talk about security. I'm afraid the Fangs of Apophis have agents in town."

A quick trip upstairs and back. On his return, he found homemade cookies and a pitcher of fruit water waiting for him. Quickly, he described the strange events at the Warren. Ariel listened, somber but unafraid.

God, how he adored her! So many women would panic, beg him to leave town, demand that he take care of everything. Ariel wasn't terrified. From her questions, short but insightful, he knew she was already planning what she needed to do to keep his family safe.

Their family. She loved them as much as he did. It seemed selfish to claim the children for himself alone, when she gave her heart to them every day. Her love, her devotion, made her the mother his children deserved.

His Alpha was right. Ariel McDunnah possessed a noble spirit. Why oh why couldn't his Dragon just Claim her?

"Did you find any clues about who these agents might be?" she asked.

"No. Though the Hares thought they'd seen Rats in town."

"Rats… oh!" Ariel's jaw dropped in shock, then she began to sputter furiously. "I am an idiot! I am *such* an idiot!"

"What's wrong?" He placed his hand upon her knee, sliding a bit closer to her.

"There was a strange man watching us today. I think he was a Rat Shifter."

Enemies here? Near my children? My woman?

With a growl that echoed in Owen's own throat, his Dragon rose. Power coursed through his body. His blood burned and light flared in his eyes, setting them afire. His skin and hands remained human, but his Dragon simmered just below the surface, ready to attack at a moment's notice.

"Tell me."

Under his burning gaze, Ariel paled. Few could stare into

the eyes of a seething Dragon and not flinch. Yet, her courage did not waver. She related the day's events, how she'd found a squalid trailer in the hills behind their woods.

"I knew there was something wrong about him, but I'm only Kin. I can't recognize Shifters when I see them. Then when you mentioned Rats, I knew what I'd missed."

"I'm going to take care of this, now," he said, rising to his feet. "Lock the doors."

"I'll be upstairs beside the children," she promised. "And tomorrow, I'm going into town and getting a proper gun."

A gun wouldn't do much against one of the warriors of the Shifting kind. Bears and Wolves would be injured by a gunshot; a Dragon, merely annoyed. But Rats weren't warriors. "Good idea." He trusted her to make sure a weapon was kept safely away from his children.

"Good luck." She stood on her toes and tried to plant a chaste kiss on his cheek.

He turned, and her kiss fell upon his lips.

A heat born of passion, not Dragon's fire, burned through his veins. He wrapped his arms around her, pulling her soft, curving body against his. Her lips parted, opening to his kiss. Betraying that her longing matched his. He savored the taste of her, the swell of her breasts fast against his chest.

Agony though it was, he forced himself to leave that embrace. Voice still rough with desire, he murmured, "I have to go."

She, too, pulled away, disappointment plain in her flushed, bright face. "Be careful."

One last touch, her fingers stroking his wrist, and she retreated upstairs. To guard herself and his children.

Owen stepped into the backyard.

Few mortals could bear to watch a Shifter change. Their minds, used to dull, mundane lives, panicked. Most fled, raving about UFOs and wild animals, unable to even recall clearly what they saw. As Kin, his child would not be harmed by the sight. However, he'd never told them about his secret life – and seeing your father transform into a Dragon was something *no* child would take well!

A quick scan showed that all the curtains were drawn. Except the hallway window, where Ariel watched.

She was full Kin. He wouldn't hide his soul from her.

With a wordless keen, Owen summoned his Dragon.

Energy from the mysterious Other Side filled him. His body expanded, Shifted. Tanned skin glittered with scales. Talons and fangs, sharp enough to shred cars, curved from his hands. He rose, looming over the pool and a great serpentine tail unfurled behind him. With a final shake, two majestic wings burst forth, spreading out over the yard.

Fully Dragon now, Owen glanced up at the window.

Would she still be there? Had she fled, fearful of the great beast he held in his heart?

No. Ariel remained. Wonder and joy filled her face, not fear. She watched, breathless, her lips parted in surprise. Staring at him in adoration.

He loved her.

That word came easily, now.

Owen crouched, then threw himself into the air. Scaled wings beat the air, whipping the pool's water into a frenzy. With strong, powerful strokes, he rose into the air and sailed toward the place where Ariel had found the Rat.

No lights betrayed its location, making it hard to find. As he flew into the darkness, however, his Dragon's eyes took over. Colors faded with the light but the night's gloom vanished too. The world became a painting in silver and black. Details stood out sharply. Not even the deepest shadow could hide a foe from a Dragon's eye.

There. Moonlight glinting off abandoned cars.

Owen circled, scanning the clearing. Shed, cars, trailer, junk… but no sign of any living creature.

Wait. Was that a woman's laughter? Coming from inside the dilapidated trailer?

He swooped to the ground, landing with a thud that shook the fragile building. At once, silence fell.

"Rat!" he thundered. "Show yourself!"

No one answered.

"Now, or I tear that junk heap in half!"

"No need for that," said a whiny voice to his left.

Owen's head whipped about. The man stepping around the trailer was indeed a Rat. To a Shifter's eyes, his form shimmered between a scrawny, ugly man and a dog-sized rodent that was even more hideous.

Out of reach, the man sidled away, circling him.

"Walker Smith?" Owen turned, keeping his eye on the devious rodent. The man was shockingly brave for a Rat; he'd expected him to bolt for the woods first chance he got.

"Yeah?"

"Why have the Fangs of Apophis sent you to Adeline?"

"They ain't. Not that I expect you'll believe that."

They'd turned a half circle now. The Rat began to back away. Owen didn't follow. He didn't need to. One leap and he could pounce on the wretched creature anywhere in this clearing. "Why did you plant mines at the Warren?"

"I didn't. I don't got *nothing* to do with them Hares. Town went to hell when they showed up."

"You expect me to believe that it's just a coincidence that they were attacked on the same day you spied on my family?"

"I don't expect that at all," the Rat sneered. "I *expect* you'll make up some crap in your head and believe that. I *expect* you won't pay no mind at all to anything I say."

The man stood there, hands balled into fists, defiant. He'd

never seen a Rat do that before. They were cowards, traitors. What was he doing?

Suddenly, he understood.

He's trying to get me to follow him. Away from the trailer behind me.

Owen turned back and studied the ramshackle structure. Was there another Rat inside? He *had* heard a woman.

He raised his foreleg and tapped a claw on the mossy roof. The trailer shook. Nothing inside reacted, however.

But the Rat did. He scampered forward, shocking Owen with his audacity. "Leave my home be. Yer business is with me."

Owen ignored him. He lowered his great serpentine head and nuzzled the trailer gently. Even that light touch set the thing rocking.

Nothing. Not a peep from within.

A sudden sharp pinch nipped his flank. Owen's head whipped around. To his shock, the Rat had produced a hunting knife and was futilely attempting to stab his rear leg. Over and over he jabbed, throwing his full weight (such as it was) behind each blow.

Not a one could penetrate a Dragon's thick scales. Of course. A fact the Rat must know.

What the hell? Can Rats go rabid?

A flick of his tail sent the creature spinning into the bushes. Owen turned back to the odd trailer…

…and as he did, the door popped open and the world went crazy.

Rats poured out, scattering in all directions. Caught in instinct, his Dragon drew back and prepared to lash out with its deadly claws. But as the blow descended, horror swept over him.

Small! They were too small!

They were children!

With a deafening roar, he reared back, fighting his Dragon. Wings buffeted, sending dirt and Rats tumbling across the junkyard. A skinny woman, her face scarred with birth marks, snatched up the smallest boy and began to crawl away.

A predator at heart, his Dragon longed to snap the vermin up. They were enemies! Foes! No matter how small!

No! We don't harm children! They're innocent!

His Dragon raged with disgust. There was no such thing as an innocent Rat!

With every bit of his will, Owen ordered it back. It howled, it snarled, it fought him, roaring with fury, for control of their body. Visions of mayhem flooded his mind. He craved battle, yearned to throw himself into the midst of his enemies and make them pay.

We do not *harm innocents!*

In the end, he won. He was in charge, not his fierce soul. Trembling from the force of that inner battle, Owen sat down heavily in the cluttered yard. Neither knowing nor caring what junk his Dragon form crushed.

The woman and children had vanished into the bushes. Only the man remained, pale and shaking, that foolish knife still clutched in his sweaty hand.

Over its protests, Owen dismissed his Dragon. Slowly, he shrank, losing his scales and draconic form, until, at last, he stood in the clearing, one man before another.

"What's going on here?" he asked.

The Rat licked his lips. "I reckon you're trying to kill me, and I'm trying not to get killt."

"I'm not trying to kill you." His Dragon rumbled a silent disagreement but Owen ignored it. "If I was, you'd be dead. Is that your family?"

"Yes."

Did the members of the Fangs of Apophis *have* families?

Ones they'd give their lives for? Because that *was* what this Rat had just done, he realized with grudging respect. He was willing to face an angry Dragon to save them.

That was *not* the behavior of a Fang...

"Why did you bring your family on this mission?"

"I told you, I ain't on no mission. I got nothing to do with the Fangs. I live here."

"You live here. Doing...?"

"Nothing!" The Rat suddenly realized he still clutched his useless knife like a security blanket. Slowly, he sheathed it. "We just live here. It's our home."

"You and your family."

"Yeah." He folded his arms across his chest and spat. "Used to be a lot more of us. I had twenty or thirty cousins in this town. But they got took and there's just us now. We hid the best, I guess."

"Took? Who took them?"

"Fangs."

"Wait. You claim that you're the Fangs' victims, not their agents?"

"Yeah. Most Rats are."

Owen's eyes narrowed. That didn't make any sense. Almost all Rats served the Fangs. A few were free-range villains, but not many.

Seeing his doubt, Walker gave a weak sneer. "I suppose you think we love the Fangs, us Rats. Well, we don't. Yeah, we serve 'em. Cause they take our families. And once a man's family's been took, what's he supposed to do?"

The thought sickened Owen. Were they truly victims, not villains? Everything he thought he knew about Rats flipped on its head.

"I'll tell you what a man does," Walker continued. "He does whatever he has to, to keep his family alive."

Owen rubbed his temple as the beginning of a headache stirred to life. "Let's try this again, shall we?"

"All right." Walker found an empty bucket, flipped it, and sat down out of arm's reach.

"You say you're not with the Fangs."

"Nope! Well, I mean, yeah, I say that. I ain't with 'em."

"But the Fangs *are* active in town."

"Yup."

"And you claim they've kidnapped your relatives?"

"Yup."

An ugly, ugly idea was forming in his head. Owen rubbed his eyes. "When did this begin?"

"Five years ago," said the Rat.

And then he confirmed Owen's worst fear. "When them Hares showed up."

CHAPTER 11

Soft as it was, the click of the back door's knob sounded as loud as a gunshot to Ariel. On noiseless feet, she glided to the top of the stairs. She'd turned on every light in the house before she came up to watch over the children. No enemy was sneaking in.

The "intruder" turned out to be Owen, not some thieving Rat. She closed her eyes with relief. Foolish, probably. Few Shifters would even dare to face a Dragon in combat. Against Rats, Owen was perfectly safe. Yet, she couldn't help but worry. If this was a trap… if there was magic…

All those worries seemed silly now, seeing him safe and home.

On leaden feet, he staggered over to the couch and collapsed.

Once more, fear raised its head. "Owen? Is everything all right?"

His eyes, always so bright, were clouded with shame. "Yeah. Family of Rats. Don't think they work for the Fangs. Not a problem."

Then why wouldn't he look her in the face? Ariel padded down the stairs to join him. "Did you find Tamar?"

"Yup." He shrank back into the couch. "Walker's daughter. He was trying to protect her."

"Owen…" She knelt before him and took his hands, so strong, so rough, in hers. "What's wrong?"

He didn't pull away from her this time. Instead, he left his hands resting in her grasp, as if her touch gave him some comfort. "I frightened them. Badly."

No surprise there. Rats were cowards by nature – and few things were as terrifying as an angry Dragon! "Did you hurt them?"

"No."

Patient, open, she simply waited until the empty silence grew too heavy for him to bear.

"I almost hurt them, though."

"But you didn't. That's what's important."

"No, you don't understand. I *wanted* to hurt them."

She slid onto the couch beside Owen and leaned close, hoping the warmth of her body would cheer him. "That's my fault, not yours. I jumped to conclusions. I made you think these people threatened your children. Of course, you wanted to hurt them – to protect us!"

"Ariel, listen to me." Now he did turn to face her, his face twisted with grief. "I almost killed innocent children. Even when I knew they were just kids, I… I nearly lost myself in my Dragon's rage. It took all of my strength to hold myself back."

Shifters, she knew, lived in the shadow of the Other Side. Every Bear, even the fallen ones who joined the Fangs, felt the urge to protect something. Dragons must be the same.

And yet, she understood his horror. How terrible must it be to feel your soul urging you to destroy innocents? No cause, however noble, could fully cleanse the taint from that emotion.

"My Alpha once told me 'A true Dragon is his own master.' Well, I wasn't."

"Owen..."

"No. I pulled it off in the end. I didn't hurt anyone. But that was mostly luck. I came so close to..." He choked, and his grip on her hands tightened painfully. "I am no true Dragon."

The shame in his voice shocked her to her core. Owen Jackson, a Dragon of the First Flight, one of the most noble and powerful Shifters in the world...

...doubted himself?

Just as she doubted herself so often. The guilt and reproach in his words was painfully familiar. She felt it every time she thought of her parents, and how 'unworthy' she was to be their child.

The difference between them was that she knew he didn't deserve any blame. Ariel threw her arms around his shoulders and drew him close. "Listen to *me* now," she murmured in his ear. "You are a fine Dragon."

"I'm arrogant, hot-headed, and selfish."

"Well... yes," she admitted. Owen startled and blinked at her. "You didn't expect me to pretend you were perfect, did you?"

That surprised a chuckle out of him. The first knot of tension in his arms relaxed under the heat of her embrace. She rested her head on his shoulder, rocking him gently. "You're also kind and generous. You're brave. You want so badly to do what's right."

Like ice melting under the spring's bright sun, he yielded to her embrace. His racing heart stilled and she felt his cheek press against her hair. "I can't control myself or my Dragon."

"You can, when it matters."

He pulled away. Not, she realized, to escape her touch, but to watch her, to study her face once more for any signs of flattery or deceit. "Why do you always see something good in me?"

"Because you *are* good!"

"My temper…"

"Your passion." His eyes widened as she corrected him. "All those things you think are flaws? They're your passion, your heart. They're the gift of your Dragon."

"But they're dangerous."

"So are Dragons."

Around her, the world faded. Cares, worries, the future, vanished. Nothing existed except this moment. Herself, and the man she adored.

"Aren't you ever scared of me?" he asked. Tense, as if he feared her answer.

"Never. You can be yourself with me. I'm not afraid of you or your passion."

With that promise, joy erased the last traces of his guilt.

"I love you," he whispered.

Her heart sang, ringing with elation. How long had she yearned to hear those words?

Sparks of cold fire lit in his eyes, the sign of his Dragon's presence. Frightening to some, perhaps, but Ariel adored the touch of mystery, of otherworldly power that dwelled in her beloved.

He pulled her near in a strong, irresistible embrace. Lips that she had only felt in dreams joined hers. The passion that had simmered in her heart for so long blazed free at that touch.

"I want you," Owen said, his deep voice rough with desire.

A nanny should be professional. A nanny would never sleep with her employer. Yet, in this moment, she wasn't his nanny. She was simply a woman – and she answered him as a woman. "I'm yours. I want you too. All of you."

Without another word, he rose and swept her into his bronzed arms. Curled against his strong chest, he carried her to the master suite with swift, sure strides and a haste born of urgent need.

His four-post bed awaited them. Owen dropped, almost tossed, her onto it. As she began to unbutton her blouse, he yanked his shirt over his head and flung it away.

Moonlight flooded through the windows, filling the room with its silvery, elven glow. At the sight of him, bathed in that magical light, her breath caught in her throat. Her fingers stilled, buttons forgotten, as she marveled at the sleek power of his body. The way his muscles flexed as he tore off his pants and threw them aside as well.

Clothes could be a pleasure to shed. A slow, teasing prelude to love-making. The loss of each piece revealing a new glimpse of a lover's body.

Not now. Not tonight. Tonight, an unquenchable fire burned within them, a desire that chafed at any delay. Still drunk on the glory of his naked body, her fingers fumbled at the last fastenings on her shirt. Owen simply tore it open, sending buttons scattering across the floor.

Ariel neither noticed, nor cared.

Eager hands tugged her pants down as she tore off her bra. Hunger drove him to careless speed and soon, her slacks joined his clothes, flung heedlessly away.

At last, her body, too, offered itself to the moonlight. He towered above her, his cock already erect, a pillar of masculine power and desire.

And yet, even as his passion reached an unstoppable crescendo, he hesitated. "Do you want this?"

She smiled, love and pride welling up within her. With

that question, he confirmed her faith in him. In his self-control. "I do."

He climbed onto the bed, straddling her, sending the heat in her loins soaring. "I may not be gentle."

"I don't care." She ached with fierce longing, a need that would not be denied. "I'm not afraid."

With that, he took her.

He swept down upon her. Covering her, claiming her. Lips, hot and greedy, found her mouth. She slid her legs apart. The heat of his body, its weight, pressed between her thighs. Rubbing against the damp eagerness of her slit. Ariel moaned, wrapping her legs around the hard, unyielding strength of his hips.

The sex of their dreams had been sweet, its fire stoked with play and teasing. But this… this was passion. This was madness. A hunger, a need, that tolerated no delays. That wanted no foreplay to bring it to climax.

Yet, even as his desire threatened to overwhelm him, Owen paused again. His hand slipped between her legs, fingers probing inside her. Seeking the wet anticipation that proved she was ready for him.

He doubted? Then she'd show him that her desire matched his!

With an impish smile, she slipped out from under him. Then, without a word, she pushed him onto his back. As his eyes widened, she straddled him, settling on the hard plane of his stomach. Surprise turned to lust as he watched her above him, full curves bright in the moonlight. His hands rose to her breasts, cupping them. His thumbs stroked her rough nipples.

Ariel arched her back. Her hair, free, whispered across her shoulders and she reveled in the love, the lust, that filled her lover's eyes.

Reaching behind her, she grasped his thick, hard cock.

Owen moaned. His hands fell away from her breasts and clutched the sheets.

Gently, she pulled him to her, letting the tip of his engorged manhood slip just inside her damp, eager pussy. Owen writhed, moaning, as she teased him. Then she lowered herself, driving his cock deep inside her most secret places. She felt him fill her, and the thick, hard girth of his shaft drove her wild.

Planting her hands on his flat stomach, Ariel rode him. Each thrust of her hips sent his manhood coursing through her. Each one drew a sharp cry of pleasure from her lips. Faster, harder, until he nearly bucked beneath her. His head whipped from side to side as pleasure took him. Fingers dug at her knees. In the depths of her passion, she never felt them.

With a cry, Owen's back arched and he exploded within her. Her own passion answered him. Moaning, she came as well. Once, twice more, she rode him, as the waves of her orgasm swept over her. Then, gently, she rose, releasing him, and collapsed to the bed beside him.

They lay panting, covered in sweat, under the moon's approving gaze.

Perhaps there were things that needed to be said. Plans to be made. Futures to decide. For the moment, though, they were content to snuggle close and fall asleep in each other's arms.

CHAPTER 12

When the morning sunlight teased him awake, Owen found himself curled against Ariel. The scent of her hair, the warmth of her body, surrounded him. He lay pressed close against her, one arm draped protectively over her shoulder. Basking in her heat, her presence, he felt his manhood swell, remembering last night's passion.

Then his brain awoke and ruined everything.

What have I done?

Ariel wasn't his Mate. He knew that. So did she, poor woman. As much as he loved her, she wasn't the woman he was destined to spend his life with. Yet, here he was, toying with her. Giving her false hope. Pledging his love to her. How could he sleep with her when he knew he'd have to send her away?

Then again, how could he not?

No man could refuse the woman he loved. How could he ignore their passion or pretend he didn't feel the fire that burned between them?

No. Owen admitted defeat as those questions overwhelmed him. Ariel might not be his Mate. Yet, he knew that, no matter how much it hurt them both, she would be his woman as long as they lived under one roof. The hunger they shared simply could not be denied.

He slipped out of bed, careful not to wake her, and retrieved his clothes.

He was the first one awake in the family and even after his shower, he was alone. He called Lorde and left a message about the Rat's claim. "I don't put a lot of faith in the word of a Rat, but I'll investigate it. If we've got a traitor, the whole Warren could be in danger."

Check-in done, and before 6:00 am at that. His Alpha was going to think he was crazy. Owen considered waiting for the rest of his family to wake, then discarded the idea. Today might be a full day, depending on what he found. Best to start early.

In the foyer, he paused. The front door was slightly ajar.

His eyes narrowed. Had someone forgotten to close it properly? Kids did have a tendency to do that. Given that a Rat lived nearby, though, that wasn't safe to assume.

A quick search of the house turned up nothing, however. No sounds from the bedrooms. No intruders in any of the other rooms. Owen decided he was being paranoid. Rats were professionals. If a Rat broke into the house, he would be damned sure to shut the door behind himself! He made sure to shut and lock the door, and thought no more about it.

THERE WERE FEW SIGNS OF LIFE AT THE WARREN WHEN HE arrived, though the curtains in Clarissa's study had been drawn open. Owen let himself in and climbed the stairs. She answered his knock – not a hair out of place and wearing a Versace gown despite the early hour.

Damn, did this woman *ever* sleep?

"Owen! You're early. I hope there's nothing wrong?" She

didn't look overjoyed to see him. There was a pinched, reserved expression he'd never seen before. Normally, she practically threw herself at him.

He followed her inside, closing the door behind him. "Got some solid leads last night."

"That's *wonderful!* You're brilliant," the Hare gushed. "You've already tracked down the Rats responsible?"

Yesterday, her fixation on Rats seemed sensible. Now, after talking to Walker, he found it ominous. "Perhaps. But first, how are you feeling?"

"Tired and banged up. Though, fortunately, makeup took care of all the bruises."

He nearly snorted. She must not be badly hurt if she worried more about her looks than her health. "That's good to hear."

Her brief smile faded and she stepped over to a table by the window. "Tea?"

"Please." Good to know that even Clarissa Lange thought 6:00 am was too early for wine.

"You're much more serious than usual," she said as she poured out the hot water. "Tell me what's wrong."

Could he? If she was innocent, the queen would be an invaluable ally in rooting out the spy. But if *she* was the traitor…

Best to be cautious. "I found evidence that the Fangs have been in contact with someone here in the Warren."

"One of my Hares is a traitor?" Her eyes flashed with anger. He couldn't tell if that was real or just a good job of acting. "How are we going to root them out?"

"Do you have files on your witches?"

"Of course. I do full background checks on all of them. Would you like to see them?"

"Yes."

Unlocking a desk drawer, Clarissa pulled out a score of

folders and placed them on the table. "Here you are. I'll scan them with you, and if there's any other information you need, you have only to ask."

That, at least, seemed like the behavior of an innocent woman. Owen thanked her and picked up the first file.

Over the next hour, the two of them sipped herbal tea and reviewed the history of the thirteen Hares of the Warren.

Well, twelve of them. He noticed that Clarissa had no file on herself. None of them seemed suspicious and so he turned his attention to older researchers. Ones that had left the Warren.

Clarissa lost interest at that point. She rose, stepped to the window, and gazed out across the lawn. Occasionally, she took a sip of her tea.

"I'm surprised that Mr. Lorde hasn't gathered a Warren to study the living Wellspring."

"Maybe he will later. Right now, secrecy is a greater concern." He shouldn't even be talking about this but, well, he'd already let the truth slip. No sense pretending the Wellspring was just a rumor.

"What I wouldn't give to be part of that," she sighed. "I'd even be willing to relinquish my title and be just a common researcher. I imagine Mr. Lorde will make his own Hare its queen?"

His Alpha had a Hare in his employ? Oh, right! Amarie, the crazy housekeeper. Owen didn't even think of her as a Witch, but she must be. "I don't know what his plans are."

"Ah. Well. Put in a good word for me, would you?"

He made a noncommittal noise. Clarissa's lip twitched and that eternal smile of hers dimmed.

"I hear that one of your Flight Claimed an Adanai."

"A what?"

"I guess you'd call her one of the Fae. They're only legends. None of them Shifted to this world; they all remained on the Other Side when the Wellsprings closed. Except one, apparently." Her simpering sweetness was curdling into something closer to a sneer.

How the hell did she know more about his Flight than he did? Owen put his folder down and leaned back, frowning. "I don't know anything about that."

"No? I've *heard…*" A mocking note crept into the queen's voice. "…that she knows how to forge weapons that can kill Dragons."

No clean Shifter would have that kind of information. Maybe the Fangs did, though. Owen guessed he might have just found his traitor.

But, if so, why was she so brazen?

Abandoning all pretenses, Clarissa began to study him with the smug contentment of a cat toying with a mouse. "We've researched that too, you know."

His eyes narrowed. "And why would you do that?"

"To use against Worms." That caught him by surprise because it made sense. Worms were fallen Dragons, monsters that chewed their own wings off. Worms led the Fangs of Apophis. If he was a Witch Hare, he'd certainly want something that could harm them.

Didn't mean he trusted this woman, though.

Clarissa continued. "We found clues in English folklore. Turns out, the Saxons had problems with several Worms back in the Middle Ages. Nicor, they called them, and wyrms. They came up with an extremely clever way to kill them."

"And that was?" He really, *really* did not like where this conversation was going. But if the Witch Queen was volunteering information, he'd listen.

"Poison. There are certain herbs that – properly enchanted – are harmless to humans but kill Dragons."

She took a sip of her tea, and smiled.

Owen's stomach lurched. Suspicion flared… yet, he felt fine. No pains or queasiness. He wasn't dizzy or confused. Surely, poison wasn't painless?

She put her cup down and opened the window. "Let me show you something. Elisi?"

From down in the yard, her chief researcher answered. "Yes?"

"We need sound now, please."

Sound? Wary but curious, he rose to his feet.

"One second, ma'am." As he reached the window, he caught a glimpse of the young Hare trotting into the barn.

A second later, a girl screamed in pain.

A girl he knew.

"Sydnee!" Owen roared.

Blazing with fury, his Dragon leaped into the fray. Magical energy flared, he began to Shift…

…and suddenly, agony tore through him. As if his insides had turned to molten lead.

Owen collapsed to the floor, writhing in pain.

Clarissa's smile broadened. "Ah, that's a relief. The Fangs let me experiment on some of their lesser Worms, of course, and I was 95% sure that it would affect a Dragon. But one worries. There's always that 5%, isn't there?"

She sat and poured herself another cup of tea as she watched his helpless struggles.

"So glad I was right."

CHAPTER 13

"*A*riel? Ariel? Can we go outside yet?"

The plaintive cry roused her from a deep sleep. One eye cracked open. Trey and Brody stood beside the bed, twin accusing scowls on their faces.

"It's laaate!" Trey groaned.

Little Brody seemed on the verge of tears. "I'm hungry!"

She started to sit up, but as the sheets slid across her skin, she remembered.

Last night. Owen. The love they'd shared.

"Why are you in Dad's bed?" Trey complained.

"I, um, I slept over." The boys looked dubiously. Sleeping in a different room of the house didn't sound like a lot of fun to them. But they accepted her excuse.

Quickly, she clutched the blankets to her chest. What time was it? 8:30? Oh, hell, no wonder she had a rebellion on her hands. The Jackson children had gotten very used to breakfast promptly at 6:30!

"Go downstairs. I'll be right there and get you some breakfast."

Normally, she fixed a proper meal. Eggs, bacon, and a

waffle or toast. Today, everything was off kilter and the boys got to indulge in their favorite sugary cereal. Kept (hidden) precisely for emergencies like this.

There was no sign of Sydnee. As the boys munched on miniature chocolate chip cookies, she knocked on the girl's door.

No answer.

The room was empty, though Sydnee's rumpled bed proved she hadn't been gone too long. Ariel wandered back downstairs. "Trey? Brody? Have you seen your sister?"

Mumbled denials.

Baffled, she glanced about. The children's shoes were lined up neatly by the front door.

Sydnee's weren't there.

Could Owen have taken her to work? Surely not, since he suspected a traitor in the Warren.

A chill settled over her and her feet, unbidden, picked up their pace. She searched the house. Nothing. A circuit of the yard gave no clues. No bodies floated in the pool. No Sydnee sat outside, glued to her cell phone. Ariel dialed the girl. No answer – and she couldn't hear a ring.

By now, her heart pounded in her chest. Even the boys, usually so clueless, grew quiet, sensing her fear. "Did Sydnee say she was going out? No?"

Time to accept this was a real problem. Ariel dialed Owen's number. Three rings... four...

"You've reached Owen Jackson. I can't answer the phone right now but..."

Ariel hung up. He'd be at the Warren by now, not on the road. There was no reason he shouldn't answer.

Unless something was truly and awfully wrong.

A corner of her mind whined that this was nothing. Sydnee probably went for a walk... Owen was busy... she was being silly... Yet, something deep inside her knew better.

Call it a Momma Bear's instinct, handed down from her own mother.

Her family was in danger. She knew it.

She had to find Sydnee.

Yet, what about the boys? She couldn't drag two little children into danger. She had no friends, no babysitters she knew in town. There wasn't even a neighbor close to their isolated mansion.

Except…

"Trey, Brody. Put your shoes on."

Six pairs of beady Rat eyes stared at her in disbelief.

"I'm sorry. I have no right to ask you, not after the scare we gave you."

"You got that right," Walker Smith grumbled. "Try to kill a man one day then ask him to watch yer kids the next. You lot ain't right in the head."

Trey and Brody gazed out at the junkyard with the rapt, joyous expressions of children on their first visit to Disneyland. Ariel knew what was going on in their heads. They longed to clamber over those junked cars, tip the ancient refrigerator over, and roll around in that rusty barrel. No doubt, she'd come back to find them covered in scrapes and dirt. A future of tetanus shots seemed likely.

Still, she had no choice. And she had no doubt that the Rats would keep her wards alive. If not clean.

As Walker and his wife whispered, she called both Sydnee and Owen again. Neither answered.

"All right." Mrs. Smith's soft voice interrupted her worries. "I'll watch 'em."

"Thank you! Thank you so much."

The first cloud of doubt dimmed the boys' mood, as they realized they were about to be left with strangers. Then a small Rat boy, about their age, stepped out from behind his mother.

"I got a buncha banana slugs in a bucket. You wanna see 'em?"

Instant bonding. Trey and Brody's joy returned at once and all three trotted off to find this amazing trove of slimy treasures.

Good. At least she could be sure they'd be safe. Ariel passed the other woman a slip of paper. "That's the number of Brandon Lorde, the Alpha of Owen's Flight. If I don't come back within a few hours, call him. Let him know what's happened."

Mrs. Smith held the note gingerly, like it might bite. Her wide, frightened eyes studied it then rose to her husband. For a long moment, the two Rats stood there, as if locked in some silent conversation.

Finally, Walker nodded. "I'll go with you. I hunt. I track well."

Relief and shame warred within her. Relief at the offer of aid. Shame because of the doubts she'd held against them. Rat Shifters were ugly as hell and their Shifted forms were downright loathsome. Yet, Walker's offer was generous. Noble, even. The sort of thing she expected from a Bear or a Wolf.

Not a Rat.

"Thank you again," was all she could manage.

He nodded. "Show me where you last seen her."

CHAPTER 14

In front of the Jackson mansion, Walker trotted in circles, his beady eyes fixed on the ground. "Yep. She come over here." Once he pointed, Ariel could see the outline of a girl's shoe on the road's dirt shoulder.

"We'll never be able to follow her," she sighed. "There won't be any tracks on a paved road."

"She didn't use the road. She crossed it." One skinny finger flicked at a clot of mud in the center of the street. "Then she took off into the woods." He nodded at another print on the side of the road and a tiny skid mark where Sydnee slipped crossing the ditch that lay between their road and the forest.

"But why? What's in the woods?"

"Dunno." Walker scrambled over the ditch and kept going, following a trail only he could see. "Guess we'll have to ask her when we find her."

That easy confidence, so strange in a skittish Rat, buoyed Ariel's spirits. Once again, she gave a silent prayer of thanks for his help.

Occasionally, she spotted one of the clues he tracked. A

broken twig. A weed, stomped flat. On her own, though, she wouldn't have made it ten feet.

Walker lasted a half mile before he stopped and crouched. The Rat seemed to fold in on himself, growing smaller, and his eyes darted about nervously.

"What's wrong?" She scanned the dense woods too, looking for any signs of Sydnee's passage.

"We got a problem. Big one," he whispered.

Ariel missed half of his mumbled words. She knelt beside him, fighting to ignore the unreasonable flash of revulsion that washed over her as she brushed against his leg. "Why?"

"Your girl, she's walking that way, straight on."

"Why is that bad? What's up there?"

"It ain't where she's going, it's how. She's walking straight as a crow flies." When Ariel didn't respond, he scowled. "People don't do that. We drift left or right. Take away our bearings and we walk in circles. Ain't natural to go straight on like this."

She shivered. "Why... no, *how* could someone do that?"

"Spell." The word sent a shiver down her spine, confirming her worst fears. "Only thing I ever seen. Fangs git something of yours 'n' put a 'Come Hither' spell on it. Then you walk straight to it. Don't stop. Don't look left nor right. Don't drift. You walk straight on."

Ariel took a deep breath, ordering her stomach to settle. "The Warren's that way, isn't it?"

"Yep. 'Bout a mile over this ridge."

Ariel pulled out her phone and tried Owen and Sydnee again. Nothing.

No weapon, no plan, no Dragon to back her up. So be it. She'd figure something out.

When she rose to her feet, Walker remained crouched low. "I ain't going in there."

"I wouldn't ask you to," she assured him. Rats weren't

fighters and there was only so much she could ask of a stranger. "But my family's in danger. I have to go."

"Suit yerself." His nose twitched violently; she half expected to see whiskers pop out of it at any moment.

"Will you do one more thing for me? Follow the trail – let's make sure it goes to the Warren. Then wait while I go in."

"That's two things," he grumbled. She waited for an answer. Walker shifted, grumbled, and finally spat. "Fine. But I ain't sticking around if it's dangerous. Don't think I will."

That would have to do.

Straight as a ruler, the trail made a beeline to the Warren. Once every doubt of that faded, Ariel pulled out her phone and called Brandon Lorde.

No one answered; her call went to voicemail. After leaving a short message, she hung up quickly, cutting short any chance of a late pick up. An Alpha Dragon like Lorde would *never* permit a mere Kin to take this sort of risk. Danger was the domain of protectors, Shifters like Wolves, Bears, or his own Kind. Not that Lorde could stop her. He was too far away and she was too stubborn. But she didn't want to argue right now.

The two of them came out of the woods behind a neatly painted barn. The yard between it and the farmhouse was dotted with cars and two U-Haul vans. Young women, arms full of boxes, staggered about.

The Warren was moving. Judging by the confusion, they hadn't planned to do this.

Good. The more disorganized her enemies were, the more time she had to figure out a plan.

Here and there, scruffy men lounged about. They didn't lift a finger to help the Hares.

"Shifters?" she whispered to Walker.

He shook his head. "Thugs."

So, how was she going to find her family in all this mess?

The Rat took that moment to remind her that she was on her own. "This is it for me."

"But you'll wait for me?"

"Til someone notices you, yep. Then I'm gone."

No apology, no excuses. It was up to her. First, she needed to know where Sydnee and Owen were.

From her pocket, Ariel pulled her cell phone and dialed Sydnee's number.

Immediately, a musical jangle rang out from the barn – not twenty feet ahead of her! Hope blazed in her heart... until a man spoke from the front of the barn.

"Who the hell keeps calling that kid?"

"Dunno," a second voice answered.

There were guards then. At least two of them. Ariel hung up.

First thug was pensive now, however. "Cops can track phones, can't they?"

"I think I seen that on tv, yeah."

"I'm gonna throw the goddamn thing in the woods then. We don't need nobody following us."

They were going to throw it in the woods *here*, where it could lead the police to the Warren? Clearly, these guys were not hired for their brains. Ariel and Walker waited as the guard retrieved Sydnee's phone and lobbed it far into the raspberries.

Once the two bruisers had settled back at their posts, she tried Owen's number. This time, she didn't hear a thing.

She didn't have a Rat's ears, though. "Farmhouse." Walker's voice was as soft as rustling grass. "Second floor. Room with the curtains open."

"Remind me never to try to sneak up on you," she whispered back. He flashed her a toothy yellow grin.

So, she knew where her loved ones were.

Now what? The barn was guarded…

No. The barn *door* was guarded. But was there another way in?

Nothing turned up in her first scan. No back door, no hatches. If they existed, they were up front. Yet, as she studied the rear wall, Ariel spotted something. A shadow in the thick grass that grew about the base of the barn.

Was that a hole? Keeping the barn between her and the kidnappers, she slunk down to the wall.

True to his word, Walker stayed behind where it was safe.

Cool air, heavy with the scent of old manure, wafted out of the grass. Brushing it aside, Ariel found what she was looking for: a small gap where a board had rotted away.

Ignoring the dank stench, she lowered herself to her belly and wiggled through it. Cobwebs brushed against her face. A rusty nail snagged her shirt and tore a two inch rip. For a moment, boards pressed against her sides, her shoulders, threatening to hold her in place. Then she wiggled free into an old stall.

No animals lived in this barn. Instead, it was crammed with junk. A rusted truck on cinder blocks. Antique tractors and farm tools. Strange, metallic things she couldn't name. All remnants of the old farm.

In the midst, tied to a pole, sat Sydnee. The poor child was gagged, her face stained with mud and tears. Ariel scurried over to her. Sydnee gave a muffled shriek, but her eyes lit with relief when she recognized her nanny. Ariel raised a finger to her lips as new tears began to spill down the girl's face.

Fortunately, the barn was chock full of sharp, dangerous implements. Ariel grabbed an old blade and carefully sawed through Sydnee's bonds. Once the girl was free, she scooped her into a hug. Thin arms wrapped themselves around her, hugging her back with a fierce love. She held the girl just long enough to reassure her that yes, it was going to be all right. Then, with a kiss on the head, she let her go. Too scared to be her usual cool, aloof self, Sydnee grabbed her hand and squeezed it tight.

She led her back to the gap. Sydnee wiggled through in a flash; Ariel followed with a lot more squirming and writhing. A minute later, they were safe with Walker at the edge of the woods.

"May have to make you a honorary Rat," he snickered.

Dirt and manure streaked her clothes, her hands, and her face, but Ariel gave him a triumphant grin of her own. "Can you get Sydnee out of here?"

"Yep. C'mon girl."

Sydnee kept her death grip on Ariel's hand. "Why aren't you coming?"

"Your father's still here. I've got to help him."

"I can help too!"

"Shush!" Walker hissed. His eyes flickered fearfully about. "Don't yowl so!"

Ariel shook her head.

"I can! I'm not useless! I…"

Let me come with you! I can help! I'm not useless!

She'd said those same words herself. To her parents – right before they left.

And died.

Ariel winced as that memory, still sharp as a razor, flooded back. Years later, the pain of their rejection had lost none of its sting. Yet, facing that same plea, she finally understood. They couldn't take her into danger with them. Not because she was 'useless.' Because they loved her too much.

Deep inside, a knot in her heart loosened. One she'd never felt before.

Momma? Poppa? If you can hear me, I'm sorry. I see now why you left me.

There was, however, one thing she would do differently. She'd use gentle words to let her little girl down.

"Sydnee, listen." Ariel kept her voice low. "I need you to take care of your brothers. Can you do that? They're all alone right now. They're probably scared to death."

Okay, that was a fib. Trey and Brody were probably entranced by banana slugs and had completely forgotten that there was anything wrong. But if it took a small lie to get Sydnee to safety, then so be it.

Weeping silently, the girl nodded. One last kiss, one last hug, and she let Walker lead her off.

CHAPTER 15

*N*ow came the hard part. Nobody was leaving a Dragon tied up, unattended. Ariel sat, catching her breath and fighting to calm her ragged heartbeat.

If only there was someone she could call on. It would take hours to summon Owen's Flight and they didn't have that much time. The local police could make it sooner, of course. Yet, what could they do against Shifters? Worse, the Fangs wouldn't hesitate to kill police officers.

She couldn't take that risk. With Walker unwilling to lend a hand, that left just her to save the day. In a fight, she wouldn't stand any chance against the Fangs. Stealth was a different matter. Owen was probably trapped by some kind of magic. If she could sneak in and break that spell, squashing a Warren of Hares wouldn't make a Dragon even break out in sweat.

If she could break the spell.

When her hands finally stopped trembling, she slipped back into the woods and circled around the Warren.

Unlike the barn, the farmhouse had a back door. Ariel

crept up to it and peered through into an empty kitchen. The handle turned easily in her hand.

Odd. Why wouldn't they lock...

Something breathed across her wrist, stirring the hairs on her arm.

Magic? Ariel froze, terrified that the spell would sound an alarm. Yet, nothing stirred inside and after a gut-wrenching moment, she scampered into the kitchen safely.

It was probably set to detect Shifters. Kin like me aren't something a Witch Hare needs to worry about.

Or so they thought. She aimed to prove them wrong.

Inside, she paused at the door to the hallway and simply listened. What she heard made her heart sink.

Footsteps. Lots of them. The Warren was a hive of activity. Hares rushed about, scooping books, papers, and belongings into boxes. The kitchen seemed to be the only room that wasn't being torn apart and stuffed into packing boxes.

How on earth could she get upstairs? She couldn't sneak past that many people. Only thirteen Hares lived here; they'd recognize a trespasser the moment they laid eyes on her.

Fear rose, threatening to freeze her in place. Ariel swallowed it. She couldn't lose her nerve. Owen's life might depend upon it.

Maybe she'd never be a Dragon's Mate... but she *was* a Dragon's lover. And she would walk through hell itself to save him.

An old wall phone hung on the wall beside her. Seeing it gave her a plan. A dangerous, awful one... but it was her only hope.

Swiftly, she lifted the receiver and dialed three numbers.

Two rings, and then: "911, what is your emergency?"

She said nothing, giving the computer a chance to register her call.

"Hello?"

Ariel hung up. Then she raised the receiver again and listened.

Dial tone.

Carefully, she placed the receiver on the counter. 911 called you back if you hung up. If you said it was a mistake, that ended things. But if they couldn't reach you…

She prayed she hadn't just gotten some innocent police officer killed. She didn't need them to rescue her, though. All she needed was a distraction.

The next fifteen minutes stretched out like hours. Time and again, she found herself on the brink of despair. They weren't coming. They hadn't gotten the Warren's address. They'd lost the call.

At last, though, she heard the crunch of gravel in the drive. Worried murmurs, footsteps. Someone ran upstairs. A minute later, a familiar voice descended the stairs.

Clarissa Lange. "It's probably that idiot nanny," the Witch Queen said.

Adrenaline poured through her and it took every ounce of her will not to bolt out the kitchen door. How could they know she was here? How had she given herself away?

"She's been calling him all morning," Clarissa grumbled. "Silly little git probably asked the police to check on him. I'll handle this."

They didn't know she was here! Knees weak with relief, Ariel grabbed the counter to hold herself up.

From outside, she heard Clarissa's honey-coated tones. "Good morning, officers. Can I help you?"

That was her cue. With all Hares at windows, eyes glued on the police, she slipped into the hallway and up the stairs. Forgotten when the officers arrived, the door she sought lay open. Ariel stepped inside. Closed the door – and locked it.

As soon as she turned, she saw him.

Owen lay on the floor, a picture of agony. Every muscle

in his lean body was stretched tight, as if caught in an unending cramp. Back arched, teeth bared in a grimace, he lay immobile.

"Owen!" She dropped to her knees beside him and laid her hand upon his shoulder. His skin burned, fever-hot, a temperature so high only a Dragon's magical blood could bear it. No ropes or handcuffs bound him. Only the rigor of those agonized, wire-taut muscles. Yet, his eyes focused on her. His lips writhed, as if he sought to warn her or beg her to leave him. Not a sound escaped his pain.

"Sydnee's safe and I'm going to help you," she promised.

Brave words. But how?

Quickly, she patted Owen down, searching for anything that could be the focus of a spell. A thorn piercing his skin. An amulet hidden in his pocket. When that turned up nothing, she scanned the room. Most of it was torn apart and dumped into boxes. She yanked open Clarissa's desk, hoping to find a voodoo doll or suspicious pouch. All she found was parchment stationery and golden pens.

One thing on the desk did catch her eye: two tea cups. Used.

Two...

Ariel sniffed one of them. It smelled of grass and odd herbs she couldn't name.

Poison? She dug through a box half-filled with vials and bottles. They were all labeled, mostly in Latin which she couldn't read. Not a one of them seemed to say anything useful like "Antidote."

Time was running out. Ariel peeked out the window. The police were still there, chatting and laughing with Clarissa. Clearly, the queen had persuaded them that this was all a mistake. A half dozen of her Hares stood by her, looking sweet and innocent.

That meant there were another six still in the house.

Ariel weighed her options. She could scream for help. She didn't doubt the police would try to save her – but she also knew the Hares would kill them. She couldn't bring herself to shed innocent blood like that.

She couldn't fight this many women. She had no help to call on. The only thing left was flight. Somehow, she had to escape, with Owen.

If she could carry him…

Ariel crouched beside her love, slipped her arms under his body, and tried to stand.

It was hopeless. She struggled, strained, called upon her Bear ancestors to lend her a fraction of their strength. Yet, she could barely raise him off the floor.

Tears stung her eyes.

I'm sorry, my love. You need a true Bear, not a useless Kin like me.

At that first touch of despair, something stirred in her heart. A passionate, indomitable love that refused to break.

You're not useless. You saved Sydnee. You can save him.

Crippling doubt withered, faced by that fiery emotion. Ariel blinked away her tears and forced herself to think.

If she couldn't lift him, she needed to drag him. Grabbing Owen's agonized body by the ankles, she threw herself backwards. To her delight, he slid heavily across the floor.

Okay, so I can *move him. I can't get him down the stairs and past six Witch Hares, though.*

Now what? A Dragon would hurl himself into battle and slay every Hare on this property. A Bear would toss Owen over his shoulder and trot off to safety. Neither option worked for Kin like her.

But a Rat…

Walker would run away. If he couldn't, he'd hide.

The closet at the end of the hall! They could hide there. And when Clarissa returned to find Owen gone, she'd probably panic. With good reason. Even an injured Dragon was a terrifying warrior.

With any luck, the Hares would flee. And, at worst, Owen's Flight must be on its way by now. In just a couple hours, this place would be flooded with angry Dragons.

All she needed to do was hide. To be an honorary Rat, not a Bear. With a little luck, this would work.

Luck, however, was in short supply that day.

She had Owen halfway to the hall closet when the creak of a board warned her that the game was up.

Clarissa Lange stood on the stairs, staring at her. Surprise and anger warred on her elegant, beautiful face.

"The nanny. Trying to stage a rescue?" Incredulous laughter spilled out.

Ariel straightened and scanned the hall for a weapon. What she wouldn't give for a nice marble statue or stray baseball bat! Again, luck deserted her. She balled her hands into fists.

"My Warren is under attack... by a nanny." Still snickering, the Witch Queen strolled down the hall toward her. "What are you going to do? Send me to bed without my supper? Threaten to tell my parents how bad I've been? Take away my dessert?"

Oh, Ariel longed for a witty comeback. Some smart, snarky retort that would wipe the arrogant smile off that woman's face.

And... she couldn't think of anything. Clarissa had a point: she had no idea what she was going to do. All she knew was that she couldn't leave Owen. Even if it cost her life, she would stay with him.

To the end.

At her feet, a violent spasm twisted Owen's tortured

body. His eyes rolled wildly as he fought the poison that held him helpless while danger stalked toward his lover. His rage, his desperate struggles, frightened even her.

How much worse would the fury of his Dragon be right now?

Too bad it was locked away inside him, unable to help.

Instinct, fierce and protective, made her step between him and the Hare. She'd shield him with her body, if that was the only hope that remained. "His Flight is on the way," she said, not sure if she was lying or not.

Her enemy merely sniffed. "We'll be gone long before they arrive. And you'll be dead."

Ariel had never hit anyone in her life. Seeing her tense, Clarissa paused well out of arm's reach. Her nose wrinkled with disgust. "A fist fight? Please."

From a pocket, she pulled a tiny gun, so small it almost looked like a toy. Despite its size, Ariel knew it could kill her.

A groan from near her feet drew both women's eyes.

Owen had rolled onto his knees. Head hanging, torn by wrenching gasps, he fought to stand.

Ariel dropped to her knees beside him and brushed his sweat-drenched hair back. His body was a mirror of pain, every muscle stretched to its breaking point. Yet, his eyes stared straight ahead, fixed on nothing she could see.

"Elisi!" Clarissa called. "Get me zip ties, *now!*"

"You think a piece of plastic is going to hold back a Dragon?" Ariel sneered. "You're doomed, all of you!" She didn't really believe that; Owen could barely stand. But if she could scare the Witches off, maybe she'd survive. Hares weren't known for their courage.

Yet, her threat didn't ruffle Clarissa in the least. "They're for you, not him."

A hand slammed down on the railing beside her. Ariel

jumped as Owen dragged himself to his feet. "Owen! Can you hear me?"

"He can hear you," Clarissa said. "He can also hear this."

A shot rang out, painfully loud in the small corridor. Ariel flinched, expecting to feel a bullet tear into her flesh. But the Hare had simply fired into the wall.

Why?

Now the gun swung toward her. "Next shot blows your nanny's head off."

Tremors swept through Owen as if the poison had suddenly doubled its efforts against him.

Suddenly, in a flash of insight, Ariel understood why the Hare was 'toying' with her.

Two cups. They both drank it. So that poison must only affect Dragons. The more he calls upon his Dragon's power, the more it hurts him.

And nothing in this world roused a Dragon like a threat to its loved ones.

Ariel's heart sank as she realized the truth. Far from saving Owen, she'd doomed him. The Hares would tie her up and torture her every time her love fought through the poison. Her pain would be the chains that bound him.

No. She'd rather die.

Without a moment's hesitation, Ariel spun and darted toward the window. It was only a one-story fall, but if she dove head-first…

A shot rang out and agony tore through her calf. With a scream, Ariel collapsed to the floor.

"How valiant," Clarissa sniffed. "Elisi! Where the hell are those zip ties?"

Ariel tried to struggle to her feet but her wounded leg gave way under her. She turned and found Clarissa looming over her. And Owen…

Owen wobbled to his feet behind the Witch.

One soft groan of pain escaped him. Clarissa whirled, eyes widening in shock. "Wait! Your nanny's hurt! She's bleeding! I'm going to kill her!"

Threat after threat spilled from her lips. Each one a dart that ought to pierce a Dragon's heart and summon its full, uncontrollable rage.

Yet, Owen stood, tall and proud.

Through clenched teeth, he hissed, "A true Dragon is his own master."

Then he drew back his fist and decked the stunned Witch Hare.

CHAPTER 16

That evening, Owen carried her through the front door.

Their home was filled with Dragons. Three tall, powerful men in tailored suits awaited them. A fourth, a more laid-back blonde with a Dragon tattoo curling around his bare arm, played with the kids out by the pool.

Ariel didn't know any of them. A regal, dark haired man rose as they entered. Judging from the deference that the others showed him, he had to be Brandon Lorde, the Alpha of the First Flight.

"Welcome home, Miss McDunnah," he said.

"Good news." Owen lowered her gently onto the couch. "The bullet didn't hit the bone or anything critical. A couple weeks of bed rest is all she needs."

"I didn't need to be carried in," she confessed. "I have crutches in the car."

"And I have arms," Owen countered, drawing chuckles from his fellow Dragons. "You won't be hobbling about on crutches while I have them."

Trey spotted her first. "Ariel!" he shrieked. Both little boys scrambled out of the pool and shot toward her.

"No running by the pool!" she cried – at the exact moment that the poolside Dragon shouted the same thing.

Someone is a father! she thought with a laugh.

Trey and Brody hustled in. Behind them, trailed Sydnee. For once, there was no sign of the girl's cell phone. The little boys launched themselves at her, and if their father hadn't warned them off, they would have climbed all over her and her injured leg. Sydnee hung back shyly until Ariel scooted aside to make room for her. Then she nestled up against her, her desperate hug proof of how much she'd worried.

Gazing around the room, she felt her heart swell with joy. Surrounded by her family, guarded by a Flight of Dragons… the world could not be more perfect.

Introductions were made, names exchanged. The boys grew bored and headed back outside, trailed by the blonde Dragon. (Morland, she reminded herself. She needed to remember their names.) At some point, one of the men grilled a batch of steaks to a perfect, bloody medium rare. A dozen foil-wrapped potatoes and a six pack of beer rounded out the meal.

Later, once the children were put to bed, the talk turned to Shifter business. Something the kids weren't old enough to hear.

"The Hares are safely in Shifter custody," Lorde assured them. "Clarissa Lange was working with the Fangs of Apophis all along. She'll be dealt with." He didn't spell out what he meant, but the grim nods of the other Dragons assured her that she didn't need to worry about the queen again. "The others will be questioned. If they've joined the Fangs willingly, they'll share Lange's punishment."

Lorde paused and took a sip of his beer. "If it's true, your Rat's testimony changes things. Previously, I hadn't considered the possibility that a Shifter might serve the Fangs against their will. I need to think on this in more depth.

"Where is this Rat, by the way? I had hoped for an opportunity to speak to him."

Both she and Owen had to smile at that. "Yeah, no," her lover said. "He isn't walking into the middle of five Dragons."

"Once my leg is better, I'll talk to him," she promised. "I'm the least scary person in this room."

The Alpha shook his head. "By that point, you'll be gone. I'm giving Jackson a new assignment. Effective immediately."

They had to leave Adeline? It hadn't even been two months, yet already she'd grown fond of the little town. Well, at least the move hit in the summer. Before the kids went to school – and before Sydnee made more friends to abandon.

Owen began to study his bottle of beer. "Where are we going?"

"I have not worked that out yet."

"Then why am I going anywhere at all?"

"Because the reason that brought you here no longer exists." Lorde leaned back, so very casual. Yet, Ariel's gut told her that he was setting a trap for Owen.

If so, her lover didn't see it. He barreled straight on, without hesitation. "I disagree. The Warren is gone but there's still a lot to do. I want to follow up on Walker's leads. See if I can find those kidnapped Rats. Plus, there's a Wellspring here. Yes, it's dormant, but it still deserves a protector."

"True, all of it. Those are worthy causes for you to pursue... *after* you fulfill your mission."

"My mission?" Owen cocked his head, confused. "The Warren's gone. I can't very well help with its research."

"That was never your goal, remember?" And with that, the jaws of the trap snapped shut. "Your mission was to find your Mate."

Ariel felt her cheeks grow warm as the other three Dragons startled. They hadn't known. They assumed that she was his Mate. That she was something more than just a hired nanny.

That cool, calculating expression never left Lorde's face. "I had hoped one of the Hares would be your soul mate. Clearly, *that* didn't work out," he added drily. "The odds of you meeting anyone in this town are miniscule. I'll see about re-assigning you to a large city. Preferably one that has a large contingent of Shifter women."

Shifter women. Ariel wrapped her arms around her chest and wished, with all her heart, that she could melt through the floor. Because what the Alpha really meant was 'someone worthy of a Dragon'.

Someone different from her.

He didn't come out and say it, but Ariel knew the truth. For one day, she'd let herself dream that this could work. Her rescue would prove her love. His Dragon would see the strength of her soul and Claim her.

None of that had happened. She'd done her best and she was still just herself. Kin, not Shifter. Nanny, not Mate.

Now grief filled her eyes with foolish tears. She was going to embarrass herself... embarrass *Owen* by weeping in front of his Flight like a jilted teenager. Dammit, where had he dropped her crutches? She needed to escape before she shamed herself. "Pardon me, it's getting late and I should..."

"Wait." Owen's tone, firm and quiet, held her. "I want you here for this. Mr. Lorde." Suddenly formal, he set his bottle down on the table and faced his Alpha. "I want to remain here in Adeline."

The room had gone quiet. Hope, that treacherous emotion, stirred in Ariel's heart.

"I don't care what you want. You have a mission and you need to complete it."

Owen's chin rose. "I decline your 'mission.'"

She gasped. Around her, the Dragons froze in place, startled by this refusal.

Lorde leaned forward, his eyes locking with Owen's. "You 'decline' an order of your Alpha?"

Unable to bear that piercing gaze, he winced and glanced away. "Please don't order this."

"But I do. I order you to find your Mate."

"No."

Soft as that word was, it was still open rebellion. Fire stirred in Lorde's eyes. "So, you defy your Alpha?"

Dragons were proud, regal creatures. Yet, like Wolves, they followed the most powerful of their Kind. Owen squirmed at the accusation; his Dragon must be gnawing its own talons right now. But despite the natural urge to submit to an Alpha's will, her lover held firm.

"I will not look for a Mate. If you think that's rebellion, so be it."

"And *I* will not trust a Dragon with half a soul!" Lorde countered.

Her stomach tied in a knot. Owen would do this for her? Turn his back on his Flight? Abandon their cause, just as magic returned to the world?

Love, pained and tender, welled up within her. He was glorious, proud... and she couldn't let him sacrifice everything for her.

"Owen, it's all right. I don't mind. I..." The word lodged in her throat, but she choked it out. "I *want* you to be happy."

"I am happy!"

Why did he have to make this so hard? "Not as happy as you'd be with your Mate. Mr. Lorde is right. This woman, whoever she is... she's your soul mate. Fate meant you to..."

Owen bounded to his feet. "Screw Fate!" he snapped. "And screw *you!*" he added, with a venomous glare at Lorde.

Ariel squeaked and clapped a hand over her mouth, sure that this insolence would summon the rage of the Alpha's Dragon. Yet, he remained seated, the ghost of a smile playing around his lips.

As his fellow Dragons tried to hush him, Owen rounded on his Alpha. "Okay, fine. I didn't Claim Ariel. We didn't have some stupid dream about cups and daggers. No mystical Dragon appeared and intoned the Rite of Claiming. And you know what? I don't care! To hell with your idiotic rituals! I love her, and I'm going to marry her."

He was… what? The blood drained from her face as she struggled to understand what he'd said. He didn't want a soul mate? She was good enough?

He loved her?

Full of righteous anger and defiance, Owen faced his Alpha, daring him to deny him.

Face impassive, Lorde studied his Flightmate. Testing the strength of the other Dragon's rebellion. And when Owen did not yield, his smile, half hidden all this time, finally broke free. "Miss McDunnah appears quite surprised by your intention to marry her. Did you plan on telling her before or after the wedding?"

"What? Oh!" Ready for a fight, the sudden 'surrender' left Owen speechless. He turned to her, saw the shock on her face, and quickly dropped to one knee.

"Ariel, will you marry me?"

Marry him? Heart and head whirled in confusion. One moment, she had resigned herself to losing him, forever. Now, he offered to share his life, his family, with her?

Of course, she wanted to marry him! But before she could even open her mouth to accept, he barreled onwards. "I love you. The kids love you. You've turned us into a true family."

"Owen…"

"I mean it! Without you, we'd fall apart. Your kindness won Sydnee's heart. Your love saved my life."

"Owen, I…"

"I can't live without you. And I can't imagine that any love, even one blessed by a Dragon, could be deeper and more real than what I feel for you. You *are* my soul mate, whether my Dragon knows that or not. I…"

She raised a finger and gently tapped his lips. "You have to let me say 'yes.'"

"Yes? You'll marry me?"

"Of course, I'll marry you!" How could the silly man ever doubt that? "I've always loved you, even when I was sure it was all hopeless."

He kissed her then. Full of passion, full of promise of a glorious future. They would always be together. Man and wife, even if not Dragon and Mate.

And that was good enough for both of them.

Farrell, a red-haired Dragon, cleared his throat then mouthed the word 'Ring?'

Horror flashed across Owen's face. "Oh hell. I've messed this up. I don't…"

"Perhaps this will do for now?" From a pocket, Brandon Lorde produced a small ring box. He flipped it open to reveal a gold band with a great diamond that glittered even in the room's dim light.

Dazed, Owen accepted it. "Why do you have an engagement ring in your pocket?"

"Because I suspected something like this would happen," his Alpha admitted. "Every time you checked in over the last month, you talked more about Miss McDunnah than the Warren."

Vexation began to burn away her love's confusion. "Then why did you give me such a hard time and threaten to send me away from her?"

"Because if you weren't willing to fight me for her, you didn't deserve her. I would know that you did not truly love her."

Owen's nose wrinkled; clearly, his Dragon was growling about the trick. But he took the ring from its holder and slipped it on her finger.

Ring... Dragon... a future together... she loved them, longed for them all. Yet, one doubt lingered.

"Are you sure this is all right?" she asked Lorde. "I'm not his soul mate."

"Are you sure about that?"

"The dream we shared wasn't the Rite of Claiming."

"Perhaps not. Though I imagine the fault is Jackson's." Owen bristled, but kept his tongue. "Only a true Dragon can Claim a Mate. Jackson is as brave and honest as any Shifter. Yet, he's been selfish and lacked self-control. Up until now," he added, as her love scowled.

"Now, he truly is a Dragon. A Protector. So who knows what the future will bring?" Lorde raised his bottle of beer in a toast. "To the new couple."

"To the new couple." The rest of the Flight joined him in that salute.

Ariel beamed and snuggled closer to her love. She couldn't predict the future any more than Lorde could. Yet, she knew that no matter what came, she and Owen would face it, side by side.

Together.

Ariel stood on the beach once more. Wind in her hair, just as in the first dream. Same ethereal gown swirling about her.

This time, however, she held a cup. A golden chalice emblazoned with a Dragon's sinuous coils.

Behind her, she heard a whoop of delight.

Turning, she saw Owen bounding over the white sands. "Ariel! Ariel!" He waved a black handled knife in the air. "I found the dagger!"

He was so excited he forgot the delicate little sash wrapped around his waist. As he charged toward her, it fluttered off.

Again. Just like in the last dream. He seemed destined never to wear that thing for longer than five seconds.

She started laughing and waggled her cup at him. That won her another cheer.

Above them, the ghostly outline of a Dragon appeared in the sky. "No Claim without Truth," it rumbled, in tones of thunder. "Show her your soul."

Her heart felt ready to burst with joy. This was it. The

Rite of Claiming. She wasn't 'just' Owen's love – she truly was his Mate!

Still chuckling, he kissed her once more.

"Let's do it right this time, shall we?"

* * *

Thank you for reading Dragon's Nanny! If you loved it then we are pretty sure you are going to love the next book in the series, Dragon's Redemption!

<u>Click here to get Dragon's Redemption on Amazon!</u>

Perhaps a little sneak peak at Dragon's Redemption? …

Lafferty's, the hottest restaurant in Jackson, Wyoming, boasted signature cocktails, aged steaks, and a Michelin star rating. Today, the entire establishment had been reserved for one purpose only.

To honor her.

Bree Williams surveyed the tables packed with tycoons and millionaires, the elite of one of the wealthiest cities in the US. They had come, decked out in their tuxedos and designer evening gowns, to toast her.

She deserved it. She'd made them all a hell of a lot of money.

Luxe Estates had just sold its last plot. Seventy-eight multi-million-dollar homes were about to be built. Elegant mansions with breathtaking views of the Grand Tetons.

How many challenges had she defeated? Well, to start with, six crotchety old ranchers, none of whom wanted to part with their land. Three zoning ordinances that had to be overturned. Four town meetings spent calming irate citizens who feared Luxe would be a glorified housing development.

And scores of title problems, each one a legal landmine that could sour the entire deal.

But she'd beaten those challenges, each and every one. Now she sat, surrounded by splendor, celebrated by the most powerful people in the state, on the verge of earning a seven-figure commission herself.

So why, she asked herself as she swirled her pisco sour, wasn't she happy?

The steak was perfect, the drink sharp and strong. The people were, well, a little tedious. Diamond-drowned elites trying to impress each other. Yet, the man at her side made up for that.

Daven Kane was her partner, the yang to her yin. A high-powered lawyer, the big gun she could always count on when negotiations failed. She sweet-talked the ranchers and smoothed the fur of the upset locals. He followed behind her. Slaying the legal problems she found. Making sure the contracts were tight and ironclad. And bringing out the knives whenever anyone tried to back out.

On top of that, he was good in bed. Lean, athletic, and willing to try anything once. Bree stole a sideways glance and admired his sharp cheek bones, the sweep of his dark hair, the way his eyes sparkled when he laughed. They were a great pair – both in bed and in the office.

So, why the melancholy?

She sipped her pisco, savoring the froth of egg whites that topped it. This always happened. She closed a deal, admirers laid the world at her feet... and instead of celebrating, she found herself like this. Staring into an expensive drink, wondering where her happiness fled.

"Don't like the drink?" Daven leaned close, surrounding her with the scent of his aftershave.

"Hmm? Oh, it's fine." Bree drew a deep breath, savoring the musky, masculine scent.

"Then why the long face? I hope it's not the company."

"No, no." She laughed and brushed his cheek with a light kiss. He waited, patient as always, until she shrugged. "I guess I'm just wondering what's next. What do I do now? Life seems empty without a project."

"Let me get this straight." His whisper was soft and warm against her ear. "Less than twenty-four hours after you close an enormous deal, and you're bored?"

"Not bored, no," she protested. "More like…"

"Hungry. Eager. Ready for the next challenge. That's what I love about you," he murmured as he nuzzled her hair. "I've never met a woman as ambitious as you. You're a natural born wolf."

High praise coming from him. Wasn't that what she'd always wanted? To be rich and powerful? To be a predator, not prey?

So, why this hollowness? This emptiness?

"Do you know what I need right now?" Bree slipped her foot out of her shoe and slid her stockinged foot along his leg.

Daven's smile sharpened, ravenous. "Right now…?"

"Yup. Right now, I need… another drink." Bree downed the rest of the pisco and waved her glass at the attentive waiter.

"Tease," he laughed.

"Well, I'll need other things later," she promised. "Just not in front of a crowd!"

The drink arrived. Then another. Then dessert (which, of course, had to be accompanied by a snifter of sherry). Then one more pisco for the road. As the speeches and toasts died out, Bree finally relaxed.

See? Enough alcohol always does the trick. Toss some good love-making on top of that, and everything will be fine.

Ting, ting!

Beside her, Daven rapped a knife against his wineglass, silencing the room with a bright, clear ring. "Ladies and gentlemen! I have one last announcement to make."

Pleasantly buzzed, Bree beamed at him as he rose to his feet. He gave her a quick nod then turned a radiant smile on the other diners. "We've spent the evening piling accolades on this magnificent woman. Now, with her consent, of course, I'd like to add one more."

Daven drew something out of his pocket and held it out before the crowd. Startled 'oohs' and 'aahs' swept across the room. She couldn't quite make out what this thing was, but clearly, people were impressed.

With a flourish, he turned and held out a tiny box. Nestled in its velvet-lined heart was a ring.

A ring with an enormous pea-sized diamond.

"I plan to make this lady Mrs. Bree Kane." Applause and cheers met his words.

People surged to their feet, clapping wildly. Only Bree remained seated, struggling to understand what was happening. Was Daven proposing? Normally, proposals involved questions not statements. But that was Daven for you. Questions gave people an opportunity to say 'no.' Better to stick to statements, right?

Could this be a joke? Bree swallowed and gazed up at him, trying to catch the glint of laughter in her lover's eyes. Unfortunately, she couldn't. Daven wasn't looking at her. His eyes swept the audience, drinking in their admiration and approval.

The diamond glittered, catching the table's candlelight and scattering it in a thousand gleams. Something that size must have set him back $100,000. It held her, dazed, like a deer in headlights. She couldn't bring herself to take it, though, and after a moment, the cheers wavered.

Only then did Daven look down at her, and his pleased expression dimmed. "Bree? You'll marry me, won't you?"

Would she? The urge to chug her pisco slammed her, hard.

Well, why shouldn't they marry? Daven was rich, handsome, and great in bed. He had ambition to match hers. What more could she ask for?

There was one obvious problem: love. Did she love Daven?

Continue reading the next story in the Dragon Dreams series, Dragon's Redemption, here on Amazon…